Love Letters and Thirst Tonics

Love Letters and Thirst Tonics

MOONVALE MATCHES

HAILEY BLACKWOOD

Author's Note

I want to make sure everyone is FULLY aware: ***Love Letters and Thirst Tonics***, while cozy and stress-free, does contain adult language and explicit sexual content.

You may proceed. (:

CHAPTER 1

Fiella

My day was perfectly normal until everything went haywire. I gulped down a mouthful of strange-flavored thirst tonic as I hustled to get ready for my day, one boot dangling from my grasp as I hopped around with the other boot unlaced.

I was running late. Again.

I glanced in the mirror and caught a glimpse of blue. I stopped short, hoping I was hallucinating. I reached toward my hair with shaking fingers. "Ugh, gods damn it!"

The thirst-reducing tonic I'd been drinking had once again been contaminated, and this time I'd wager it was with bluebells. The seasonal flowers were lovely, sure, but when combined with the magical properties of the tonic, they tended to cause strange side effects. Like blue hair, apparently.

The strands on my head were as blue as the afternoon sky. Brighter, even. They practically glowed.

At least the color suited my complexion well enough,

and it would probably fade in a few weeks. Kizzi must have screwed up her potions again. I'd have to give her a piece of my mind the next time I saw her.

I was just relieved that the ache in my throat had been soothed.

As a vampire, even a half-blooded one, I'd been pestered by the incessant thirst for blood since I was a wee little thing. It was a pain in the ass, but it was nothing I couldn't handle, as long as I kept purchasing those overpriced tonics from the apothecary shop in town, Kizzi's.

Even though Kizzi was supposedly my best friend, she wouldn't give me a discount. Traitor. The trinket-selling business was dreadful during the freeze season and my silver stash was uncomfortably light. I couldn't seem to catch a break!

I usually tried to think positively, in a goblet-half-full kind of way, but it was getting harder and harder with every bump in the road.

My parents had moved away from Moonvale a few years ago to "travel the lands", and their absence was a constant ache in my chest. I missed having them around.

Shit gets lonely around here.

I liked to think of myself as a badass, independent woman who didn't need anyone, but *gods. What's a vampire gotta do to find someone to share a lavender blueberry cider and a few kisses with?*

My cottage was a mess, as usual, but it was one of my happy places. I had moved into my haven as soon as I could afford to live on my own, and it had been the best decision of my life. It was small, but it was cozy, and it was *mine.* Every available space was filled with houseplants. I had a massive bookshelf filled with tomes covering the entire side wall, and I even had space for my personal collection of knick knacks. Trinkets filled every nook and cranny. It was delightful.

There was hardly room for a bed among all the wonderful clutter. My bed was more of a pallet, wedged in a corner, forgotten until it was time to catch some sleep. I didn't usually pay it much mind.

I wouldn't go as far as to call myself an interior decorator, but I knew a good trinket when I saw one.

I lovingly caressed the leaves of my purple ficus as I passed, making a mental note to wipe the dust off them later. That mental note would probably vanish as soon as I walked through the door, but it was the thought that counted. I was a good plant mom when I remembered to be.

I pulled my mess of blue hair back into a twist, tucked it under the hood of my cloak, and tromped towards town. The journey would only take a few minutes, but I was determined to escape the eyes of the locals. The human and non-human folk of Moonvale were used to my antics at this point, and it took a lot to surprise anyone, but this stylistic choice had been inflicted upon me against my will. So I chose to rebuke it.

My cottage was nestled into the edge of the Greenwood Forest, and I loved the privacy that the location granted me. Sure, neighbors were fine, but nothing was better than some peace and quiet. I meandered my way through the sparse trees on the forest's border until my boots clacked on the stone walkway leading into town.

I took a deep breath, pulling crisp air into my lungs,

relishing the morning. It smelled like greenery and living things. The best smell in all realms. Or maybe the best smell was fresh-baked berry tarts—it was a very close competition.

It was still the freeze season in Moonvale, though the beginning of the mild season was slowly creeping in. Most folk seemed to be indoors, much to my luck. The only living beings I passed that noticed me were the local critters. The chirping of birds, the rustling of leaves, and the squeaking of rodents betrayed the presence of the small creatures that often scurried through town.

As was my daily ritual, I stopped by the bakery to pick up tea and a pastry on my way toward the town square. The bakery was always lively—packed to the brim with folk securing their warm beverages and snacks for the day. The scents wafting from the propped-open front door were divine, making mouths water and stomachs growl of any passersby.

I secured my bounty without any fuss, only receiving a few sideways glances that I could easily ignore. I avoided any unnecessary conversations just to be safe.

Raising my mug of tea to my lips, my fangs gently tapping against the pottery, I inhaled the sweet, earthy scent of herbs and berries as I let the hot liquid trickle into my mouth, only mildly scorching my flesh in the process.

There's nothing better than hot tea on a chilly morning.

I picked up my pace and made my way over to Kizzi's, deciding to visit my best friend and show her what her tonic had done to me before starting my own workday.

~

"Ooh! New look? I love it!!" Kizzi shouted when she caught a glimpse of my new cerulean strands, her bright green eyes flicking up to examine me. She set down her cauldron stirring rod, fixing her undivided attention on me for just a moment before she moved on to fussing with an assortment of baskets.

I glared at her. "Nope. This one's on you, not me." I pulled my hood back to reveal my hair in all its glory.

Her jaw dropped when she looked at me again. "You've got to be fucking kidding me!" she whined. "I could've sworn I finally had everything sorted out! Those sprites must be breaking in after dark again. I am *so* sorry."

The usually brightly tempered woman was frazzled, bouncing around the shop like she couldn't find a place to settle. Her smock was dirty, hanging from her curvy figure like a sheet instead of accentuating her form like it usually did. Her olive hair hung limply over her shoulders.

Kizzi had been tormented by the local forest sprites for ages now. The troublemaking creatures wanted nothing more than to cause a little mischief. I didn't know what she could've possibly done to earn the ire of the harmless woodland creatures, but they created problems for her at every opportunity.

"It's alright, Kiz," I mumbled bashfully, any frustration draining out of me immediately at my friend's guilt. My desire for justice evaporated. "It gives me a bit of a striking quality, doesn't it?" I was missing my caramel-colored strands desperately, but I didn't want to make her feel worse than she already did.

Brightly colored hair wasn't rare in Moonvale, nor was it frowned upon. I didn't even dislike it, truly. I just didn't appreciate it being inflicted upon me unexpectedly. I reached up to snag a piece that slipped free from its twist, twirling it around my finger.

Kizzi hesitated for a bit too long, and then blurted out, "of course it does! I couldn't look away from you if I wanted to! You're as hypnotizing as the moons." She quickly turned around so I couldn't see the expression on her face.

I sighed. Kizzi sure knew how to lay it on thick. I came here to give my best friend a lecture for her carelessness, but I couldn't manage to stay mad at her.

"The sprites are giving you a hard time again?" I asked. "I thought they had finally moved on after you performed that ridiculous ritual and sang to them for four hours straight." I hadn't even been able to stay in the shop during that spectacle. I loved Kizzi but her voice was worse than a siren with a sore throat. She was an impressive natural witch, but her magic clearly didn't spread to her vocal cords.

"I thought so, too," she muttered with a glumness she couldn't quite hide. "They only stayed away for a few weeks. I've done everything I can think of to shake them! They're determined to ruin my life, for no gods damned reason! I must have angered the Old Gods somehow."

I didn't know why Kizzi bothered to acknowledge the Old Gods. They had abandoned our realm centuries ago, and I doubted they had even an inkling of an idea what was happening here now. They were surely long gone. All they had left behind was remnants of magic. Mere crumbs of what used to be.

"They better keep their grubby hands off of my thirst tonics," I grumbled. "Those tonics are the only things keeping me from losing my mind and sinking my fangs into the locals." There were quite a few vampires in Moonvale, and we all struggled with our thirst from time to time, but some of us needed pharmaceutical assistance more than others.

Drinking blood straight from the vein had become an outdated practice with all the magical and medicinal intervention that was now possible. It was *taboo*, or whatever those fussy old vampire elders said. Unsavory. Frowned upon.

Vampires could find sustenance from any type of blood, critter or creature, but the blood of other vampires was the most potent. It staved off the cravings for the longest. The blood of any folk, from orcs to elves and everywhere in between, could satisfy a craving for days. A week, if we were lucky. But we were encouraged not to indulge in that delicacy.

Not unless we were mated—or willing to risk being shamed. The side effects of drinking straight from the vein were often... uncontrollable. And inappropriate.

And extremely fun, with the right partner.

Thirst tonics certainly helped with the cravings. Most days, a juicy blood-infused cocktail was just as satisfying as a few gulps of blood fresh from a living being.

Or at least I told myself it was.

"Yeah, yeah, I'm doing my best, Fi," Kizzi grumbled. Fi

was a nickname that I didn't allow freely. Only those who deserved it earned the chance to call me Fi. The rest of the realm called me Fiella. Or Miss Elmwick, if they were trying to sound fancy.

Kizzi had, like me, been suffering from the recent lack of tourism that the freeze season caused. All of the local businesses in Moonvale had. We depended on the folk of the entire realm, Aldova, to spend their silvers to keep us afloat.

The freeze season kept wanderers from other towns at bay, and only the warming of the air would bring flocks of visitors back again.

If folk couldn't travel by river boat, then they had to trek the Barren Lands, and that was a whole miserable journey and a half. I couldn't blame anyone for not wanting to endure that.

Only the desperate ever risked it.

"If those little sprites keep giving you a hard time, let me know and I'll come in here and give them a piece of my mind!" I insisted with as much wrath as I could muster. My willowy frame wasn't *that* intimidating, but I liked to think that I could strike some fear into my enemies if I set my mind to it.

Kizzi cast a skeptical glance my way, which I tried not to be offended by. She didn't know the ferocity I was capable of. I didn't know either, to be fair, but I was sure it was buried down within me somewhere.

"Thanks, you badass vampire, but I'll deal with it," Kizzi stated, not very convincingly. "One of these days, I'll figure out what their problem is."

Our conversation was interrupted.

"Hello, uh... Is there any thirst tonic for sale here?" a deep voice boomed from across the room. I practically jumped out of my skin.

"Gods! The sprites must have stolen my door chime too," Kizzi exclaimed with a hand pressed to her chest as if she could slow the pace of her heart with pressure alone.

I glanced over to see who had the audacity to interrupt this *clearly* important conversation. If they were intruding, they better at least be worth the diversion. I hadn't even gotten the chance to bite into my pastry yet or tell Kizzi about the new book I had started reading!

My eyes landed on the figure by the front door.

Oh.

Oh.

Well, I certainly did *not* expect *that*.

The being in front of me could best be described as... vast. The man was massive, taller even than my lanky frame, which was a rarity around here. He was rugged as though he worked outside throughout all the seasons, and his skin was toasted to show it. His hair was luscious and tree-bark colored, and I had the strangest urge to walk up to him and run my hands through it.

Down, girl.

My daydreams came to an abrupt halt as soon as the handsome hunk opened his mouth again.

"Is anyone actually working here or are you two just going to stand there? I don't know if you heard me, but I need a thirst tonic. I am really in a hurry here."

My jaw dropped at his bluntness. How *dare* he.

Coming into Kizzi's shop and giving her attitude? Absolutely not. Luckily for Kizzi, her self-designated protector was here.

I was a monster before I had finished my morning tea and pastry, and I was already on edge. This man had no idea what he had just stumbled into.

CHAPTER 2

Redd

I didn't know what I had done in a previous life to deserve this. This was my worst nightmare. There was no way in Hell's Realm that this was actually happening right now.

I was late for my newest work assignment, I was miserably thirsty, and now I had managed to piss off some folk I had never even met before.

I couldn't shake this streak of bad luck.

The two women I could see stared at me with matching glares.

"Are you fucking kidding me!" the taller of the two women screeched at me. I could catch a glimpse of blue hair peeking out from under the hood of her cloak. How interesting.

"You storm into Kizzi's shop and demand immediate attention—who do you think you are, the gods damned King?" she continued, waving a mug of tea threateningly in my direction but somehow managing not to spill any.

I pinched my nose between my thumb and forefinger

and suppressed a heavy sigh. I did not have the time or patience for this right now.

I tried to wrangle my irritation and plaster a semi-convincing smile onto my face to salvage whatever I could of this situation. I wasn't in the mood for a fight, and this lovely Hellbeast seemed determined to pull me into one.

"I was told this establishment had some thirst tonic for sale. I just need a dose or two and then I'll get out of your hair. Do you have any in stock?" I asked in as calm a voice as I could manage, flashing my fangs in another smile that I hoped didn't look too much like a grimace.

Of the two women, I wasn't sure who to aim my question to. The scents of many magical folk were mixed within the space so I couldn't determine the species of my apothecary companions without getting closer.

I held my breath as much as I could, just to be safe.

I usually kept myself heavily dosed in thirst tonic to avoid any annoying urges to sink my fangs into the throats of those around me, but since moving to Moonvale I hadn't managed to replenish my stash. I had only been in the area for a handful of days and had been so busy, I hadn't wandered very far into town. I was now completely out.

My rental cottage was on the outskirts, tucked into the forest, which suited me just fine. There were no neighbors to bother me. I only ventured into the town square when absolutely necessary.

One of the women, the shorter of the two, scurried behind the counter. She tilted her chin up politely and met my eyes, though her smile seemed a bit forced. Her skin and hair had a slight green tint to them, which wasn't necessarily abnormal for some of the species living in this hodgepodge town, though it was unexpected. Like the underside of a leaf.

Where I came from, Sunhaven, everyone was always at least lightly sun-broiled from the intense heat of the dual suns.

"Hi there, I'm Kizzi. This is my shop as I'm sure you already know if you looked at the name plastered on the sign out front. Thirst tonic, you said?" she chirped. This woman was entirely too lively this early in the morning. Up close I could smell the spicy remnants of magic on her–she must've been some sort of witch. My throat twinged.

"I have to warn you... I do have some thirst tonic in stock, but it might cause some unexpected side effects. You see, the sprites like to make my life a living Hell's Realm. I can't guarantee your thirst quenching won't also come with color changes, hoofed feet, or shimmery skin. It'll certainly soothe your thirst, though, I'm sure of it! Well, at least mostly sure!"

Maybe she spelled herself to never run out of things to say.

I registered her words and groaned internally. *Shimmery skin? You've got to be kidding me.* I couldn't hold back the sigh this time as I glanced around the room, considering my options.

My gaze landed on the other woman, who was glaring daggers at me from a few paces away. That sure was an impressive glare–I could respect it. I liked to consider myself an excellent glare-giver myself. Why she was glaring at *me* though, that part was a mystery. And that outburst a minute ago was uncalled for. All I had done was walk in.

Sure, I could've been more polite, but the burning in my throat distracted me from any niceties.

Was my presence so unbearable, even to strangers? Gods damn. Folk used to actually like me. Or at least tolerate me without much of a fuss.

"You know, we were having a conversation which you so rudely interrupted when you stormed in here and started making demands," the blue-haired woman grumbled at me. I could practically see steam coming out of her ears. Watching her face while she spoke, I caught a glimpse of sparkling white fangs nestled behind her plump berry lips. I quickly glanced away.

Vampire, then. Or at least part vampire.

The apothecary owner, Kizzi, interrupted her friend's tirade. "Fi, you're being a grouch. Go finish your breakfast in the back room and quit trying to scare away my new customer."

Fi. That was an interesting name. Seemed rather drab for such an intense creature. Kizzi turned back to me expectantly. Gods, I was thirsty, but there was no way I was going to risk something embarrassing like *shimmery skin*. Or worse!

I'd have to endure the acidic burning of my throat until I could snag some thirst tonic from somewhere else or wait for some trustworthy tonics to be brewed by this strange, green witch.

"I'll have to pass. I can't walk around looking like a jewel. I'll come back later and see if you have proper tonics mixed by then. Thanks anyways." My already sour mood dropped another increment.

Being thirsty sucked. It was bad enough that I was here

in this cutesy town where most folk were so obnoxiously *friendly*– adding thirst to that just made me want to crawl into bed and never come out again.

I wished everyone would just leave me alone. It was better that way. For everyone.

I caught a delectable scent as I passed the blue-haired vampire, and it was a punch to the gut. My mouth filled with saliva and my fangs ached so deeply I felt it in the bones of my jaw.

I shoved my hands into the pockets of my tunic and strolled out the front door without another word, and without acknowledging the comments from the two unusual women in the apothecary. I had clearly annoyed them and had made it even worse by not buying anything.

My job site was only a few minutes' walk from the apothecary shop, but the air was brisk enough to bring goosebumps up on my arms.

I kept my head down, ignoring the folk meandering around town and minding my own business.

I was used to the warm, dry but blanketing air of Sunhaven, and I couldn't fathom why anyone would want to live somewhere *cold*. The chilly air was so uncomfortable, it even made my fangs hurt.

Unluckily for me, I was working outside today, on some broken porch steps at one of the local orc's cottages. The thought of being in the cold all day made my already sour mood drop closer to misery.

I accepted the fact that today was going to *suck*.

My gaze was snagged by one of the old stone mailboxes on the corner. The decrepit things were all over the realm and hadn't been used since the Old Gods abandoned us ages ago. They were ancient, stone-colored, and made of a strange brick and mortar. Most of them were hardly standing upright, they were so neglected. This one was in better shape than most.

They say that the mailboxes used to be used as an easy way for folk to instantly send letters and small parcels back and forth. They were everywhere, on practically every street corner in every town of Aldova. Without the rich magic of the Old Gods, the linking enchantment had crumbled, and there was not enough magic left to support the infrastructure. So now, they just rotted.

Letters and parcels were now delivered by hand, by critter, or occasionally they could be magicked from place to place if a magic user felt like expending that much energy, and if the folk felt like paying a boat load of silvers.

Taking a closer look, I noticed that there was a sign propped on top of this mailbox with writing scrawled onto it.

For you, sweet, lonely soul. Drop your thoughts into the box and find companionship.

I snorted. Ha! How ridiculous. I was supposed to put my personal thoughts into a crumbling box that wasn't even functional anymore and somehow that was going to give me a friend. Unlikely.

It was probably a prank from one of the local littles. I didn't need friends, anyways–I had plenty back home. Well, I had a few... but they were enough. I rolled my eyes and continued on my way to my job site.

I didn't need to make any friends here in this town. This situation was temporary, and I'd be leaving anyway. It was pointless to put down roots that I would need to eventually tear free.

I made it to my job site, dropped my toolbox onto the ground, located the wood that had been delivered, and got to work, sorting through my mental checklist of tasks I needed to accomplish before the day was over.

At least now I could pour all my focus into my hands and let the muscle memory take over. I took a deep breath, pulling in as much air as I could before letting it rush out of my mouth, past my aching fangs.

The orc wasn't home, so there would be nobody around to interrupt me.

I measured the orc's broken stairs, mentally calculating how many wooden slabs I would need to chop to get this project accomplished. The stairs were larger than I had expected–the treads clearly customized for a very tall folk.

I pulled out my saw and began the laborious task of slicing through wooden planks, putting my body weight into it. I welcomed the familiar ache in my shoulder as I sank into the rhythm, the grating sound of shredding wood strangely soothing.

At least this part of my day would be somewhat manageable.

CHAPTER 3
Fiella

After the rude *but alarmingly handsome* vampire left the shop looking dejected, my thoughts were conflicted. The man was impolite, absolutely, but I knew how irritable thirst could make a vampire. I had felt the same way many times. Many, many unfortunate times. That was no excuse to be rude, though.

I hadn't seen the man before–I would surely remember a face like that. Those moody eyes and strong jaw would be hard to forget. *What in the realms is he was doing in Moonvale?*

I tugged on a strand of my blue hair, idly twirling it around my fingers. The side effects of the thirst tonics weren't *that* bad, he was just being a pansy.

I shoved the nameless stranger from my mind.

I pulled my breakfast pastries from my satchel, tossed one over to Kizzi, and dug into the other. Raspberry scones today. Delicious. She missed the scone and it plopped to the floor before she managed to pick it up, but luckily it had been wrapped in parchment.

I ignored her withering glare as I licked the sweet berry glaze from my lips.

I planted myself at a work bench and kicked my feet up, trying my best to contain my crumbs and avoid touching anything that could be poisonous.

"So, Kiz," I said around a mouthful of scone. "What's new? Besides the whole sprite fiasco thing, anyway." I swallowed, washing the bite down with a mouthful of tea. The perfect combination.

"Nothing much different than yesterday, to be fair," she answered, her own cheeks also full of pastry. She caught a berry before it could fall to the floor, tilting her head back and dropping it into her mouth. "All I've done since I spoke to you last was experiment with new ingredients for skin illuminating potions for a few hours and then catch some sleep. Oh, and I left out a very nice offering to the sprites too. Maybe they will appreciate the knitted socks."

"Ugh, how boring!" I joked. We spoke constantly, but we told each other *everything*, no matter how dull. "Let me tell you about the new book I started last night, then." I waggled my eyebrows mischievously.

"Yessssss you know I love hearing about those masterpieces. Please tell me it's a raunchy one." She sat up straighter.

I rolled my eyes. "Kizzi, what kind of lady do you think I am? Of course it's a raunchy one."

She snorted. "Right, we're the fairest ladies of them all. Now spill."

So I did. I told her about the elf maiden, and how she was trapped at the top of a magical tower with no way to escape. I told her about the handsome orc soldier who had come to save her. Kizzi's jaw dropped further and further the more I spoke, and I hadn't gotten to any of the *really* naughty bits yet.

"He did *what* to her?!" Kizzi exclaimed, looking equal parts intrigued and horrified when I told her what the soldier had done to the maiden when she tried to run away from his clutches.

"You heard me right," I responded sagely.

She shivered. "Go on, then."

I decided it was time to hold the theatrics and head on my way when a customer walked in, asking about a tooth whitening polish and interrupting my sordid tale.

I stood up with a huff, brushing the unavoidable crumbs from my lap and grabbing my satchel from where it had settled on the ground.

"Alright Kiz, I better head to the shop. To the moons!" I called out as I headed to the door.

"Yeah, yeah, sure, to the suns, Fi," Kizzi responded distractedly, having already moved on to grabbing the ingredients she needed for her customer's purchase.

The phrases had been our signature salutation since we had been littles, when we used to insist that we loved each other to the moons and back and argue over whether the suns or the moons were farther away. The phrases had shortened over time, but they had stuck.

Whether Kizzi liked it or not, she was stuck with me forever. That's what best friends were for!

~

My shop was only a short distance from Kizzi's, and the walk flew by. I hardly even had time to register that it was cold enough to make me shiver, and that abnormally few folk were out and about. It felt like only seconds had passed before I arrived at my destination.

Taking in the wood and brick of my shop building brought a smile to my face. My cottage was my home, but my shop was my haven. My paradise.

I spent more time in my shop than I did in my cottage. I even purchased a bed for the lofted area above my shop so I could sneak away for naps during slow days.

Just being at my shop was enough to lift my spirits, no matter what else was going on, and on a good day, being here made everything even better. I had painstakingly collected every single item and curated the collection perfectly.

I had procured ancient tomes from the far reaches of the realm, animal sculptures from nearby towns, and even a few hand-painted pottery sets from across the sea. The most eye-catching things in my shop were the colorful tapestries slung across the walls and hanging from the ceiling. I had collected a tapestry from every single town I had traveled to, and they gave the shop a warm, comfortable atmosphere.

I wasn't proud of myself for much, but I was proud of myself for this. Extremely proud.

Nothing gave me greater satisfaction than providing a customer with exactly what they were looking for. Folk really underestimated how much a perfectly placed trinket could transform a space, and I was an expert at finding them. My wares were the items that could turn a cottage into a home. Into a space of comfort and personality.

Humming to myself, lost in thought, I fished around in my satchel for my iron set of keys. The pesky things always sank to the very bottom, under my abandoned pastry wrappers and spare writing utensils.

An annoying presence itched at my senses, enough to mildly irritate my nose.

After fumbling around for a few seconds, I finally pulled out my iron key and jammed it into the slot.

At the first crack of the door, I caught a whiff of an acrid scent so strong it made my eyes water. It wasn't anything I had ever encountered before, and it was *foul*. It reminded me of something between rotten vegetables, animal waste, and the cleaning solvent Kizzi used to clean up stubborn spills.

The scent smacked me in the face with the force of a stampede when I pulled the door open wide. *Gods! What died in here?*

I yanked my tunic up over my face and braced my hand on the door frame to steady myself, though my lungs tried to rebel. It took a few minutes before the smell had dissipated enough to make entering my shop bearable. With shaking legs and trembling nerves, I entered. Slowly. One step at a time.

I took a quick glance around and everything seemed fine.

Surprisingly, there weren't any rotting carcasses in the middle of the room. Thank the gods.

The comfy sitting nook in the corner still had all of its seats in place, and the yellow cushions looked as fluffy as ever. The shelves full of trinkets were still spread throughout the place as they had been when I'd locked up last night. Even my plants looked bright and vibrant, their leaves slowly inching toward the light coming in the front windows.

My worktable was where it had always been. Even the jar of flowers I had purchased yesterday were still in full bloom, right where I had left them.

Nothing seemed abnormal. Maybe I was just imagining the smell? I wasn't sure my brain was capable of conjuring up something so *rank* but the tonic could have really been messing with me.

Still, my eyes burned, and I kept my nose covered.

Shrugging off my apprehension and trying to convince myself that the tainted thirst tonic was giving me olfactory hallucinations, I propped the doors open to let the lingering smell out, whether it was real or not.

My eyes dripped with tears. I wiped them away, annoyed, as I made my way over to my worktable to get everything organized for the day.

I trailed my fingers over the shade of a beautiful, beaded lamp that I had recently added to my inventory, rescued from a small, dusty shop in the beachy town Tidegrove. The salesperson hadn't even put up a fight when I haggled with her, and she sold me the beauty for an extremely low price. A score that still made me smile when I thought about it.

I tucked away my spare pastry in the cubby below my worktable, pulled out my sales ledger, and set out my favorite quill and ink. I needed to update my inventory logs today.

"Sookie!" I called out.

Sookie usually greeted me right as I walked in the door, and I should've noticed earlier that she was missing. The smell had thrown off my rhythm. Perhaps she was taking a nap. That critter really loved naps. A quick glance around the room proved that theory false. There were no furry bodies curled up on any cushions, or on my bed in the loft.

Sookie came and went as she pleased–nobody could keep that adorable beast contained if they tried. I had learned that lesson the hard way.

Sookie was my second-best friend, behind Kizzi, of course. Sure, she was a cat, but I was convinced that she had the soul of an old, wise witch. I didn't have proof of that, but it was a longstanding theory. I seemed to gravitate towards witches.

Regardless, she was excellent company.

Shrugging off Sookie's absence, trying not to let it bother me too much, I got to work.

Before I made much progress, I caught a flash of movement from the corner of my eye. Quick as a crack of lightning, I managed to turn in time to see a beetle about the size of a silver coin darting into one of the cracks in the mortar of the floor. *What in the realms...* As I looked around and peered closer at my shop, I realized I could catch hints of the blasted insects everywhere. A reflection of a shell here, legs squeezing into a crack there. The place was crawling with them!

I never had a pest problem in the past. Sookie usually took care of that for me, so to see the place swarmed made my stomach churn and my blood pressure skyrocket.

I *hated* bugs.

In the midst of my panicking, I heard a massive *crrrrrrrack*. And then another. And then another. Plumes of dust filled the air as my shelves began collapsing, dumping my priceless collection of treasures onto the stone floor.

NO!

No, no no no no no!

A guttural scream of horror ripped its way out of my throat.

I darted around like a hummingbird trying to rescue any falling items that I could, but my effort was futile. Every single shelf in my shop collapsed! Even as fast as I was, I only managed to catch a potted orchid and a small set of woven baskets.

I found myself surrounded by the ruined remains of my priceless collection of goodies. My heart cracked into two.

Frozen in shock, I was only stirred into motion when the sound of wood cracking began again, this time from above my head. *Shit, the roof is coming down! Fuck! Fuck fuck fuck!*

I had a split second to act, and I barely made it outside before my world came crashing down around me.

I allowed myself to feel the soul-shattering panic and despair for only a few heartbeats before I sprinted into the town square as fast as my legs could carry me, headed towards the only folk I was sure could help.

I bypassed Kizzi's, as she always took house calls and made deliveries at this time of day, and she would surely be on the far side of town. I ran past my other neighbors as well, because there was nothing they could do for me in this chaos. I needed the mayor's help. He would know what to do.

Seconds later, I burst into the mayor's office, red-faced and huffing.

"Mayor. Tommins. I need. Your help," I puffed out between gasps of air. I really needed to start working out more, this was kind of embarrassing.

Mayor Tommins was a gryphon, and younger than I'd always expected mayors to be. He had been the mayor for as long as I could remember, but he never seemed to age a day. I had no idea how old he really was.

I was clearly interrupting his morning as he jerked his eyes up to look at me, startled, with his mouth hanging slightly open. His pointed teeth caught the light. It took him a moment to shake himself free of his stupor and register what I had said.

"Miss Elmwick, I can see you are rather flustered. What in the realms is going on?" he asked, setting down the parchment he was reading and rising to his feet.

"My shelves!" I heaved, slowly beginning to catch my breath. "They've collapsed! All of my trinkets are on the floor! I've been sabotaged! The whole place is coming down!"

Mayor Tommins didn't seem as shocked by this information as he should have been. Why wasn't he panicking? This was a travesty!

I was sweating buckets, and my hands wouldn't stop shaking. My breaths wouldn't slow. It took all of my will power to hold off the wave of panic that was threatening to rise and pull me under.

He took a moment to gather his thoughts before

answering. "I'm sorry, Miss Elmwick. That is very unfortunate. I am afraid to say that you aren't the only Moonvale resident having problems this morning. There has been a string of incidents over the past few days. It seems we have all been having... rather poor luck."

Luck! This had nothing to do with luck. Sturdy oak shelves didn't just collapse for no reason. Someone was *clearly* out to get me. "I need help! What can you do? Are any earth witches or builders available to come take a look? Everything I've got is in there. Everything!" I leaned on his desk as I began to feel lightheaded, nausea churning in my gut.

The mayor sighed deeply and slid his glasses off so he could drop his face into his hands. "I'll add you to my list," he mumbled between his fingers. "We'll get someone out there as soon as we can. It might take some time. As I said, you aren't the only one with a disaster right now."

"Okay... okay. Yes, please, just send someone whenever you can." I couldn't hold back my wave of disappointment. I wanted to fix this *now*.

I stifled a huff of frustration, thanked Mayor Tommins, and left the office. I was proud of myself that I only stomped a *little* bit. I wanted to throw a full-blown tantrum. My entire livelihood depended on my shop, and if I couldn't keep selling trinkets and earning silvers, I was absolutely screwed.

My shop was *everything*.

I had kept Fiella's Finds afloat for five years, since my Ma had handed it off to me during my twentieth year, and I would be damned if I'd watch it crumble now. I had poured all my blood, sweat, and tears into that place.

I came from a long line of trinket sellers. I had learned from my Ma, and she had learned from her Ma before her. The business had passed through generations, but I had morphed it into something that was entirely my own. My project, my vision, *my shop*. Trinket selling was in my blood. It was my passion, my joy, my life's mission.

Pa was a painter, but he had been by Ma's side back when the shop had been called "Moonvale Novelties", and they ran the business together. They had both retired and moved on to exploring the realms, but that didn't mean I was going to let the shop crumble to dust now that they were long gone (current situation notwithstanding).

The walk back to my shop took much longer than my panicked sprint to Town Hall, but it still passed much too quickly. I wasn't ready to face the damage behind the green-painted door. The tremors in my hands turned into full-blown quakes as I reached for the handle, dreading the closer look I would have to take at the damage.

At least most of the structure seemed to be remaining upright. The back corner had collapsed, but the remaining three were holding on by a thread.

Thank the gods for brick reinforcements.

Water pooled in my eyes and my throat constricted. My much-too-rapid breaths caused my vision to begin tunneling. Panic was slowly sinking its deadly claws into me, creeping under my skin and into my muscles. Crunching my bones.

If I opened that door and witnessed the destruction inside, I feared that the fragile tether I had on my emotions would snap.

I stuck the key into the lock, sweat trickling down my back, between my shoulder blades.

I gritted my teeth and pulled the door open just a crack. An inch. Two. A beetle scurried out through the gap and over my boot. I squealed, slamming the door shut and leaning against it. The walls creaked ominously, and I immediately straightened up, my whole body shaking.

That was tomorrow Fiella's problem.

Tomorrow, I will be strong enough to handle this.

Tomorrow, I will face it.

Tomorrow.

For today, I am allowed to feel weak.

I locked the door back up.

Alcohol. Alcohol was what I needed right now. I needed to numb myself, to dull the sharp blade of pain that was gouging into my heart.

My keys clattered to the ground as I tried to tuck them back into my satchel. I tossed my head back, shoving my fists into my eye sockets and using any willpower that I had left to hold myself together.

My voice trembled as I muttered to myself, "I'm not going to cry. I'm not going to cry. I'm not going to cry."

I snatched my keys off the ground and headed over to Ginger's Pub with my heart in tatters and my spirits in the gutter. It was time for a drink. Or five.

CHAPTER 4
Fiella

Ginger's Pub was one of the liveliest places in Moonvale. The pub was in the town square, right in the middle of the action, and there was *always* something entertaining happening there. Folk could celebrate with a bubbly ale, wallow in misery with a jug of wine, or simply sip on a cider and enjoy a bowl of stew, if Ginger prepared any that day.

I was determined to drown my sorrows and do some intense wallowing. A pity party, if you will. I craved the numbness, the wool pulled over my senses, the brain fogging that alcohol would bring.

I was pretty sure I was in some sort of shock. I had stepped outside of my body and was just going through the motions, my head stuffed full of cotton and half-formed thoughts.

I made my way to the bartop, plopped down onto my favorite stool in the corner, and waited for the barkeep to head my way. Ginger wasn't working the bar today, which was a massive bummer. The faun woman always managed to lift my spirits with her easy-going manner and upbeat attitude. Instead, I was being served by one of her employees—a massive, moss-brown-skinned orc with a rather impressive beard.

When the orc, Tandor, finally made his way over to me, I was barely holding it together. It took every ounce of my mental strength to keep my eyes from welling up and spilling over. I gritted my teeth, my fangs digging into my lips with the pressure.

As a very emotional vampire, I was no stranger to managing my feelings, but I wasn't always the best at it. If a few tears managed to slip free, I hoped nobody would judge me too harshly.

It happened to the best of us.

It happened to me pretty frequently, if I was being honest.

"Hi Tandor. A large goblet of today's cider, please," I requested with a slight wobble in my voice. My throat was tightening up and I was trying to breathe through it. Inhale, hold. Exhale, hold.

"Sure, Fiella. One moment," Tandor responded, eyeing me with a slight furrow between his eyebrows.

Tandor placed the goblet in front of me with a tentative smile and a request to let him know if I needed anything else. Lavender blueberry was the cider flavor today. The goblet was so heavy while full of liquid that I had to use both hands to lift it to my mouth.

Ginger's Pub catered to all sorts of folk, with many strange offerings on the menu. Bugs for the fauns, raw meats for the shifters, flowers for the druids. Blood for the vampires. The considerate orc barkeep had added a shot of elk blood to my goblet. I took a huge gulp. Delicious.

Ciders were my absolute favorite, and lavender blueberry was the best flavor of all. The sweet, fruity drink was the superior alcoholic beverage, and nobody could convince me otherwise. Ale tasted like piss water. I wasn't necessarily saying that ale drinkers liked the taste of piss but... if the boot fits.

Wine was great, but it just couldn't top the light, refreshing deliciousness of cider.

As I sipped my cider and stared off into the distance, I tried to stop myself from sinking down into my thoughts. I packed my emotions down with as much force as I could and focused on the mystery of it all. What in the realms was happening to my shop? The more I thought about it, the more I became convinced that this was a targeted attack. No other alternatives made sense.

Nothing natural could cause such abrupt destruction, such total devastation. Those beetles weren't just mortal wood mites, they were something sinister. Something dark.

Who could *possibly* want to destroy my shop, my entire life, and maybe even the entire town? What if I wasn't the last victim, what if I was just the first? What if Kizzi was next? What if the entire town was slowly crumbling to bits?

I was spiraling.

Maybe I gained an enemy somehow. I might not have been the nicest vampire *all* the time, but I always gave kindness a decent effort... at least when it was deserved. I wasn't *that* big of a bitch; Kizzi was a way bigger bitch than me.

I could only think of a few folk who might have a vendetta against me. There was that other vampire girl from back in school, I'd accidentally (on purpose) drank her bear blood lunch, and I just knew she'd never forgiven me for it. There was also the older witch woman who sat in the park and watched everyone all the time, she was always giving me the evil eye.

It could've been Josten. Fuck Josten, that asshole cheated on me and still threw a fit when I dumped him. Or maybe that book vendor from the town over. He always hated when I haggled for a better price.

The more I thought about it, the more folks I came up with. The possible enemies were everywhere. I could've made an accidental enemy out of *anyone*. Fuck, this wasn't good.

I finished my goblet with a heavy swallow and a deep sigh before Tandor immediately set another one in front of me—no questions asked and only a slight nod thrown in my direction. Good man.

I was halfway through my second goblet (and only beginning to descend into a mental breakdown) when I started daydreaming about food. The shop catastrophe had happened only a few hours ago, surprisingly, and it was now midday. And I'd left my extra pastries tucked under my shop counter. They were surely smashed to dust by now.

Another tragedy in itself.

At least I'd taken my dose of thirst tonic this morning—adding thirst to the mix would have sent me plummeting over the edge.

My pondering was interrupted when the barstool next to me was pulled back with a *screeeeeeech* against the sticky stone floor. Ginny really needed to mop this place more often.

My head a bit swimmy from the booze, I glanced over my shoulder where my elbows were propped onto the bartop to see an angel sitting next to me. Velline was newer to town, and I had only spoken to her a few times in passing. She was quiet, but kind, in a gentle sort of way. Her presence was soothing. She seemed to keep to herself. I respected that–folk were exhausting sometimes.

She let out a sigh as she plopped onto the stool. "You went blue?" Velline asked quietly. "Cute."

I simply nodded in acknowledgement, threading my fingers through my roots and tugging lightly. I was not in the mood to explain the magical mishap that I'd swallowed this morning.

Velline had been working at the healing clinic in town, Moonvale Medical, ever since Old Man Wilbur had gotten too old to run the place by himself and found an apprentice. The elf was so old that nobody could keep track of his age anymore– it was likely somewhere around seven hundred.

As non-human folk of Aldova, most of us weren't necessarily immortal, but we were pretty gods damned close to it. It wasn't abnormal for folk to live to see a thousand turns of the seasons. Some races lived longer than others, of course, but with the advancements of magical tonics, lifespans were becoming longer and longer.

In Old Man Wilbur's case, I had a feeling he was just ready to move on to something new. Like my Ma and Pa had been.

I shivered at the reminder that I would eventually have to let them know what had happened to Fiella's Finds.

Velline politely ordered a bright wine, and immediately

swallowed a massive gulp when the goblet was placed in front of her, delicately coughing when the liquid rushed down her throat. She must have been having a tough day. Relatable.

"That delicious, huh? I'm more of a cider or dark wine lady myself but I might have to order one of those," I joked, trying to lighten her mood. I was also trying to distract myself from my own glum thoughts.

Velline glanced over at me while her silver cheeks flushed a deeper gray. "Excuse my poor manners, Fiella. I don't usually guzzle wine like a fish, but I needed to take the edge off today." She took another impressive swallow, her hands gripping the goblet so tight I feared it would shatter.

I nodded at her in solidarity. Sad girls had to stick together. "I hear you there. I'm having the same sort of day. Something bad happen?"

She dabbed at her mouth with a napkin before answering. "You could say that." She had hollows under her eyes, and her usually bouncy white hair was flat around her face. Her tunic was wrinkled and stained with a few mystery substances. It was shocking to see her looking so noticeably frazzled.

Even her wings, usually fluffy and bright, hung limply off her back.

"Wanna talk about it?" I asked gently. I didn't want to talk about my own situation yet. With the alcohol in my system, I was positive that I would start weeping hysterically. I was surprisingly holding it together so far and didn't want to push my luck.

She shook her head and held out her goblet. We clinked them together, chugged them down, and set about drowning our sorrows out together. *Misery loves company, or so they say.*

Drinking with someone else was certainly better than drinking alone.

Eventually, after two more goblets and a few subtle tears wiped on the back of hands, Velline started talking. She explained how the clinic was having a strange influx of sick patients who had mysterious illnesses. Her hands were full, and she was exhausted.

I bought us another round of drinks. She needed it almost as much as I did. I didn't have many silvers to my name, and I would certainly be completely broke by the time I figured out what to do with my shop, but this moment felt essential. My coffers were already hurting, they wouldn't notice this expense.

We drank on.

Somewhere between drinks five and six, Tandor set bowls in front of us, stating that the servings of stew were on the house. I dug in gratefully. I scarfed the mixture down so quickly that I could hardly taste it, my thoughts bubbling and churning dizzyingly.

I couldn't find the courage to explain my situation to Velline. I was sure the news would spread eventually, and for now, I was just grateful for the company.

With unsteady legs, I hoisted myself up and tossed my arm around Velline's delicate shoulders. She was so short that she tucked under my armpit perfectly.

"I think it's time for me to go—one more goblet and I'll be crawling home. Bye, Velline!" I leaned on her a little harder than I intended to, but she kept us upright.

"I think that's a good idea. I need to get home too." Her

words were slightly slurred. "Thank you for the company, Fiella."

"Any time, honey! We both needed it. I hope your–" I gestured my hand around vaguely, "–*situation* gets better."

She stepped out from under my arm as we exited. "Yours, too. See you later. Get home safe!" She turned in the opposite direction, walking more steadily than I expected her to.

I meandered towards my own cottage. I really did *not* feel like being alone at home, and I missed Sookie desperately. The thought of my heavily pillowed bed, my collection of thimbles, and my prized ficus usually brought me peace, but right now they just made me feel sad.

The moons were high in the sky when I glanced up. I had spent longer than I thought inside the pub. Night had fallen and the air was chillier than I had expected–crisp enough to seep through the drunken fog clouding my senses.

Kizzi would surely be asleep by now, and I couldn't bring myself to wake her. This late, there was nowhere else to go. We really needed some businesses for the night-dwelling folk of Moonvale.

The brisk wind smelled like icy leaves and a shiver went down my spine. I loved the freeze season. I preferred it when I was bundled up in front of my fireplace with a book in hand, but it was pretty nice if I was properly dressed for it while out and about, too.

The problem was, I was *not* dressed warmly enough today. This time of year was typically warmer and I hadn't bundled myself with my knits and feather-stuffed puffy cloak.

I yanked my thin hood up around my ears, ducked my head, and speed walked towards my cottage. Running was one of the things I hated most in life–I only did it when absolutely necessary. Speed walking was *much* more practical.

I was so focused on reaching my destination that I hardly paid any attention to my surroundings. I was making great progress until I suddenly found myself sprawled on the ground with my feet knocked out from under me, my face fortunately missing the cobblestones and smashing onto the grass lining the walkway. *What in the realms?*

That was going to leave a bruise. Or ten. The pleasant buzz in my system was dulling my nerves but I knew I'd feel that one tomorrow.

Ouch.

I yanked my hood off my head so I could pinpoint my attacker, prepared to knock someone out. Oh. It was just one of those old mailboxes. Whoops. I could've sworn I was zooming in a perfectly straight line on the walkway.

Those mailboxes were so ugly and crumbly. Someone should really fix them up, or at least knock them down if they weren't worth the effort. It was a shame to watch them slowly rot away.

Grumbling, I got myself back onto my feet. Mustering as much balance as I could, I lifted one leg to deliver a revenge-kick to the mailbox to hopefully dismantle it once and for all when something caught my eye. Was that... a sign?

CHAPTER 5
Fiella

I leaned closer, squinting through my slightly blurring vision to read the message atop the stone box.

For you, sweet, lonely soul. Drop your thoughts into the box and find companionship.

I stared at the sign for a long moment, trying to determine if the message was *actually* meant for me. I *was* pretty lonely, after all. And sweet.

I had already hit rock bottom and lost everything that I cared about–I had nothing left to lose.

I didn't make a habit of ignoring signs from the fates. If this message was literally going to knock me onto my ass, I'd better listen to it.

"Huh. Well alright fates, if you say so!"

I made my way home, shivering but without any more incidents.

Gods, my cottage was such a mess! I wasn't always a messy folk, but I tended to get sidetracked easily. I lit a lantern and went on a search mission. I didn't have the silvers to pay for fancy enchanted lighting anymore, so I made the old-fashioned fire lanterns work.

I was pretty sure I didn't have any envelopes, and I hadn't seen my nice parchment in ages, but I had to have some sort of paper somewhere.

Ah ha! There it was. *That'll do.*

The paper had seen better days, but a few wrinkles and splits were no big deal.

I cleared a space on the table, shoving aside everything in my way, and pried open my old jar of ink.

Then I started writing, as fast as my drunken mind would allow. My hand only wobbled a little bit, and I only spilled the ink twice.

Dear Mysterious Entity in the Mailbox,

Hello, I answered! I'm half convinced that this letter will just rot away in the mailbox, but just in case someone finds it, I sincerely hope you enjoy this glimpse at my thoughts, because I am not in a position to mess with the fates.

It's your lucky day I guess!!! But not mine.

Are you a ghost? Are you a spirit? Are you a folk? I simply must know. I am just a regular 'ol folk, but I would make a great ghost. I would love to haunt people. I bet nothing bad happens to ghosts, except for the dying part that makes you a ghost... I wonder if ghosts can just be born as ghosts. I need to ask someone about that.

Anyways. Hey ghost/spirit/folk, have you ever felt like screaming into the void until your voice gives out? That's how I'm feeling right now. I have had an absolutely _TERRIBLE_ day. The worst day I have ever had. Or at least the second worst day. It's hard to rank shitty days, you know.

I'm worried that my life might be ruined. I know what you're thinking, "This person is so whiny and dramatic!" well, whoever you are, you might be right, but you must understand. My entire life has been destroyed today, and I don't know what I'm going to do.

Thank you for reading, mysterious mailbox spirit. (if you are actually reading and this letter isn't just going into the abyss...)

P.S. Zero alcohol went into the writing of this letter, by the way. None. Not a drop. Not even a few sips.

P.P.S. I wonder if anyone is actually going to read this.

S pilled ink seeped over the corner of the messy paper, but I didn't have the patience to fix it. I brushed away what I could, tidying up with a stray cloth.

Proud of myself for so eloquently expressing my thoughts, I bundled up in my cloak, slipped back outside, and scampered over to the mailbox–watching my feet carefully this time so I would stay upright.

Gods, those ciders *packed a punch*. I dropped the letter in the box, made my way home, and then got myself into my bed as quickly as possible. My swirling thoughts were darkening around the edges.

Mind full of mailboxes, mysteries, and magical spirits, I slipped off into a dreamless sleep.

CHAPTER 6

Redd

G ods, I was so drained. This town was a mess! I was okay with my job–I loved working with wood and creating things with my own hands, but sometimes a vampire just needed a *break*.

And I was still *so thirsty*.

Maybe being shimmery wouldn't be *too* bad. Could a shimmery vampire still be tough and fearsome? If my throat tightened up any more, I'd have to risk it and find out. Maybe I'd get lucky and end up with harmless temporary hoof feet, or something interesting like sunset-orange eyeballs.

The only way to *truly* satisfy the thirst was to drink directly from the vein, but that practice was outdated in modern times. Apparently, it used to be extremely common when the Old Gods still roamed the realm. I didn't under-stand why our elders had frowned upon drinking fresh blood. These days, blood sharing only really occurred between serious romantic partners, often mates, and we were expected to stay quiet about it.

43

It had been ages since I had indulged in the delicacy, but I longed for the feeling of hot, fresh blood sliding down my throat. My fangs pulsated at the thought.

Thirst tonics and supplemental critter blood just about did the trick, though. It was good enough.

I had been run ragged in the days since I had ended up in Moonvale and had Mayor Tommins put me to work wherever they needed help. Why this gods-forsaken town didn't have a woodworking shop was a mystery to me. They certainly needed one.

All the local handyfolk had been in a frenzy trying to keep up with all the recent destruction that was being caused. Pipes had burst, homes had slid off their foundations, and fires had started. The town seemed to be falling apart.

Just like Sunhaven had been when I left...

Nobody knew exactly what was causing all this destruction. Some of it appeared to be magical, but the reasons were a mystery. The cause wasn't any of my business, as long as I got my silver payment at the end of the day.

It had nothing to do with me... hopefully.

I dropped into Mochas & More for my blood chai latte on my way to the mayor's office at Town Hall. My body didn't require much more than a few swallows of blood to function, but the stuff was delicious and helped take the edge off the razor-like pain in my throat. It eased the cravings infinitesimally.

Almost all vampires in existence these days had some non-vampire ancestors, and we were able to survive off a combination of food and blood. Most of us needed both, sometimes one more than the other.

Unluckily, my family was almost entirely vampire, which meant we suffered the consequences of thirst deprivation more acutely than others.

Blood chai lattes were one of the highlights of my day here in Moonvale. The barista was extremely efficient and hardly spoke two words to me. It was awesome.

"What'll it be today, boss?" I asked as I entered Mayor Tommins' office. I never knew what to expect when I reported for a new job assignment. This town liked to throw me curveballs. I had only been here for a week and the experience had certainly been... unique.

Mayor Tommins was slumped over his desk, his golden hair greasy and his eyes dull and droopy. He looked like he hadn't slept in days. Maybe he hadn't. "There's been some sort of shelf collapse at the trinket shop in the town square, it's the one on the corner across from that giant tree. Just read the signs, you'll find it. It's rather impossible to miss. Do what you can, please."

He didn't even look me in the eye as he spoke, his gaze wandering to somewhere off over my shoulder.

Another day, another problem. It never ended. "Yes, boss," I responded, not wanting to stress the gryphon out any more than necessary.

Sipping on my latte and trying to get my thoughts in order, my tool bag tucked against my hip, I made my way to the square. It was nice to be able to walk this entire town. There was rarely the need for horses and carriages or other transportation methods like there was back in Sunhaven.

My family ran a woodworking and building shop in Sunhaven, and we were all involved in the business. It was lively and busy, but nothing was ever surprising. Everything was scheduled and planned and thought out ahead of time.

This current predicament was taking a lot of adjustments. I felt knocked out of alignment.

I quickly realized which shop was my destination, as it appeared to be sinking into itself. The sign on the front was long gone but I could reasonably make assumptions, based on the crumbling facade.

Collapsed shelves, my ass. This whole place has collapsed.

I sighed and finished off my blood chai with a huge swallow.

I pushed open the fragmented door and made my way inside, catching a whiff of death and grease remover in the air. *Gross, this place stinks.* There was a pleasant, and mildly familiar scent of warm skin and berries lingering that made my fangs prickle, but it was being suffocated in dreadful fumes.

It looked like a tornado had ravaged the place. When I had heard about the broken shelves, I had pictured a minor mess. A few boards that would need replacing. Something I could fix in just a few hours.

The situation before me was overwhelming. The destruction was so widespread I couldn't even tell if the floor was made of wood or stone.

The place smelled sickeningly putrid, and a thick cloud of dust particles hovered in the air. Everything was wrecked. Destroyed. I didn't know if anything would be salvageable.

I couldn't prevent my astonishment from escaping from my lips. I grumbled, "Nope. No way. Absolutely not."

CHAPTER 7
Fiella

My brain felt as though it had been pummeled with an iron rod, stomped on, and then pummeled once more.

I'm never drinking again.

I had shown up to my shop with two extra pastries in hand, determined to at least make a dent in the disaster. I had cried my eyes dry this morning while telling Kizzi what had happened and thought I had no tears left, but apparently, I was mistaken.

This travesty was enough to rattle even the most solid of souls. The waterworks continued. My cheeks were salty and raw, and probably bright red. But every time I had pulled myself together, some new wrecked discovery pulled the tears out of me once again.

I mean, come on. My adorable stuffed critters were *squashed*. My hand-carved stone mixing bowls were shattered *on the dirty floor*. And worst of all, my tiny shelf of vintage miniature books had been absolutely annihilated.

There was even a chilly breeze coming from the collapsed corner, disturbing the papers fluttering about.

At a glance, it seemed that nothing had survived the destruction.

At least Sookie was back. She must've been hiding somewhere yesterday. I couldn't blame her–that was a mess that no living being should witness. For the millionth time, I wished that she could speak so she could tell me what in the realms had happened.

I sighed, trying to regulate my breathing.

Sookie wasn't really *my* cat, but I liked to think of her that way. She had wandered into Fiella's Finds a few years ago, found a comfy napping spot in the sitting nook, and started regularly returning ever since. She even followed me home to my cottage when she felt like it.

I didn't know what she did when she wasn't around, but I was sure that it was mischievous and delightful.

She was mommy's little angel and I loved her to bits.

Sookie was curled up on her favorite plush chair, watching me weep and work while her tail flicked back and forth. She was clearly on edge. Every time another beetle scurried by, the hair on her fluffy gray back bristled up, like she was disgusted by them.

Girl, me too.

There were a lot of cats that roamed the town, and they all seemed to decide where they wanted to live and which folk they wanted to befriend. For small furry critters, they were rather persuasive. And occasionally intimidating.

Kizzi had tried to convince me to let her help, but I knew she couldn't afford to miss any days of work with so many customers demanding potions and tonics from her.

She had to stay afloat and stock up for the tourist season, and I refused to let her business suffer just because mine was. Besides, someone had to make enough silvers to pay for our pastries.

I was on my hands and knees, trying to gently extract a decorative tree sculpture from the wreckage with snot and tears streaming down my face when I heard my shop door swing open.

Mumbled words drifted toward me, not loud enough to understand from the distance.

Shit. I guess I forgot to flip the sign to *closed*. Did this idiot not have eyes? Perhaps they couldn't see the mountains of ruin and rubble.

Heavy footsteps halted right inside the door. A masculine voice called out, "Hello? Is anyone here?" I heard another mumble that sounded an awful lot like, "You've got to be kidding me..."

That voice. I knew that voice. Not *him*. Ugh! Thirst tonic guy!

I temporarily abandoned the tree sculpture and hauled myself to my feet, dusting my hands off onto my overalls. I tried to hold in my sniffles and wipe up the mess on my face with the back of my arms, but it was useless. This was a disaster.

The towering vampire looked like he had been slapped in the face. He was frozen, looking around with a mystified expression as though he had just seen a ghost.

Ghosts really weren't that scary, I'd seen plenty. He was being rather dramatic.

"Yes, I'm here, I survived the avalanche, It's a miracle!" I called in a watery voice.

I carefully made my way to the front door since there was no way in Hell's Realm that this guy was going to be able to walk any further without crushing something valuable.

"As you can see, I'm closed. So unless you're here to help, please, for the love of all things magical, don't take another step." It would be my last straw if something survived the collapse only to be squashed by this vampire's massive, booted foot.

He stared at me for a moment, looking vaguely confused. "Fi?" he asked.

Oh *hells* no. "Excuse you!" I exclaimed. "Only my closest friends are allowed to call me Fi, and you are *not* one of them." I crossed my arms across my chest, trying to put out *don't fuck with me, I'll bite you* vibes. I thought it was working. "You may call me Fiella, like everyone else." I sniffled again.

The vampire continued to stare at me for a few seconds too long before he seemed to remember where he was, shaking his head. "Right... right. Sorry. I just heard... nevermind." He cleared his throat. "Mayor Tommins assigned me to rebuild some shelves here at the trinket shop, so here I am. But there's no way shelves are being rebuilt right now, this place looks like it's been run through by air sprites and then stomped on by an Old God."

Very helpful observation, asshole.

"Pardon me?" he asked, taken aback. His heavy eyebrow quirked slightly.

"Oh, did I say that out loud? Whoops..." It really was an accident. Sorta.

Redd

It just kept getting worse and worse. When Mayor Tommins told me I needed to go rebuild some shelves at the local trinket shop, I did not expect to walk in on something like *this*. I pictured a few broken pieces, not an absolute mountain of madness.

The whole structure was caving in on itself.

Not to mention the distressed state of the vampire running the shop. This was the woman who had screeched at me like a banshee at the apothecary yesterday.

Now, she was standing in the corner, covered in dust, looking like someone had just kicked a puppy in front of her. Twice. Most of her vibrant hair was twisted into a knot on the top of her head, the rest was sticking out wildly or plastered to her neck with sweat. She looked... kind of adorable–in an intimidating sort of way, of course. I didn't know what to say to her. She was also cursing at me. Again.

I couldn't stop my mind from straying to the worst... Was this disaster my fault? I had seen her yesterday, after all.

No, no, it can't be my fault. I left all that behind me, it can't have followed me from Sunhaven...

I shook my head, clearing away the worrisome thoughts.

It would be impossible to rebuild anything right now, but with the way Fiella's lip was quivering, I was afraid to say that. She had clearly been crying and I didn't want any fresh tears to start.

I hated tears. I didn't know how to handle them.

"Okay, let's think about this. I've been assigned to rebuild your shelves but it's clear that a *lot* more work is needed here. Days, maybe weeks of work."

She sniffled.

"First, you need to get rid of those beetles, or they'll just keep destroying everything. What are those things, by the way? Is that why this place reeks? I mean, no offense or anything. I'm sure you smell lovely, er not lovely, that's not what I meant, I mean–" I cut myself off with a sigh. "Nevermind. Care to explain what in the hells happened?"

She let out a watery exhale. "I've clearly been sabotaged. It's these weird beetles that smell really bad. It's not me, I swear. Sookie killed a few, I think. I'm leaving them in a pile until I come up with a better plan," she explained, moving aside a broken chair and a ragged rack of quilts.

I shifted my weight uncomfortably. "Right... Okay. Okay. There's a lot to process there."

"A lot to process!" She snorted. "You're telling me. Gods." She wiped her face off with a scrap of fabric. It looked like it belonged to the shade of a lamp, but I kept that observation to myself. "Okay well, I guess you should stay there for now. Don't you dare step on anything important."

"Wouldn't dream of it." I stared at my feet helplessly, afraid to even move a muscle.

She began delicately digging her feet through the wreckage, taking the path of least resistance in my direction. "So, Mayor Tommins sent you? Nobody else was available, huh?"

I glanced at her blankly. "Were you expecting someone else?"

"Well, yes, actually."

I blinked, taken aback. "Sorry to disappoint."

She rolled her watery eyes as she nimbly climbed over a large, mangled globe. "I didn't know you existed until yesterday, don't get your knickers in a twist. I guess if you're all they've got, we'll make it work."

"Wow, you really know how to make a man feel special."

"If you want to feel special, talk to your Ma."

She kept wiping her arm over her face as she spoke. Was that snot on her sleeves? I acted like I didn't notice–I didn't want to make anything worse than it already was.

"Anywaysssss. I think they're magical beetles. How in the realms am I supposed to get rid of magical beetles? Kizzi, of course... But she's so busy..." She seemed to be talking to herself more than she was talking to me.

At least her voice seemed steady now. Phew.

She muttered something about needing to go to Kizzi's apothecary, clambered deftly through the piles of junk, and walked right past me and out the front door. Okay, then.

She paused a few paces down the road and looked over

her shoulder. "Oh, by the way, you haven't told me your name," she stated matter-of-factly.

"That's because you haven't asked," I retorted. Because she hadn't.

I opened my mouth to tell her regardless, but she shrugged and walked away without another word, hustling toward the apothecary shop I had seen her at yesterday.

I shook my head, mystified. What a beguiling creature.

I could have headed back to Town Hall to get a new work assignment for the day–I was sure there was plenty else to be done, but instead, I decided to stick around and start cleaning up.

Tragedies happened everywhere all the time but... If, by the slimmest chance, it was my fault that this disaster had occurred, then the least I could do was try to fix it.

I tucked my tool bag beside the front door, rolled up my sleeves, and got to work, smashing a beetle under my boot as it tried to scurry away. The crunch made me shiver with revulsion.

Yuck.

CHAPTER 9
Fiella

I felt much better once I had a mission in mind.

Step 1, convince Kizzi to help me get rid of the demon-spawn beetles, but without impacting her business in the process.

Step 2, clean up my shop enough that the vampire stranger can start rebuilding my shelves. *I really need to figure out his name at some point.*

Step 3, rebuild and reorganize.

Step 4, sell everything in the shop, get rich, and never have to work again in my life unless I want to.

Goblet-half-full, or whatever.

I burst into Kizzi's shop desperate for some help. I knew she would have my back, as she always did, but I didn't know if her magical expertise would extend to beetle extermination.

"Kiz!" I shouted as soon as I caught sight of the witch behind the counter. Thank the gods there weren't any customers in the shop today, I didn't want to make a habit of scaring away her clientele.

We all needed as many customers as we could get during the slow season.

I didn't waste any time getting straight to the point. "I need your magical brain to figure out how to get rid of wood-munching beetles!"

Kizzi just stared at me for a moment. "A quick *hello* would have sufficed, but I suppose that works too." She set a bundle of herbs on the counter and dusted her hands off on her thighs. "I've been thinking about this since you came into my shop this morning, but I need all the details. You didn't really explain much when you were blubbering on my shoulder, which is totally understandable, by the way! I'm not judging at all. I'm just saying. Explain, please."

I did. I told Kizzi everything, even including the parts where I drowned my sorrows in lavender blueberry ciders and encountered the nameless vampire with my face smeared in snot.

Kizzi's face filled with compassion as she absorbed my story. It wasn't that I didn't like pity, because who didn't like to be the center of attention every once in a while, but coming from my best friend, it made me feel squirmy.

What I needed was some help and a kick in the ass to get things fixed.

"Girl... no offense, I know you're having a delicate moment right now, but that's so embarrassing," Kizzi said. Her hand pressed over her mouth muffled her words. "That guy was pretty cute too! Rude, but cute!"

"Don't remind me," I grumbled. It was bad enough that anyone had seen me during a humiliating low point. The fact that the guy was an asshole and a hottie made it a million times worse.

"You're lucky your best friend is a magical genius!" Kizzi proclaimed. She was many things, but humble was certainly not one of them.

Kizzi went on to explain to me that, while she didn't have all the necessary ingredients to create a fumigation brew, she knew exactly where to find them.

I didn't ask for all the details, because I didn't understand most of what the witches got up to, but I trusted her to handle it.

"Will you bring me one of those beetles when you get the chance? I'll get it to the coven so we can start investigating," Kizzi asked.

"Now how in the realms am I supposed to do that? Just pick it up and carry it in my hand?"

She flapped a hand in my direction. "I don't know, Fi, figure something out. Use that beautiful brain of yours."

"Whatever. Sure, sure. I'll bring one of those demon-spawn beetles over as soon as I can."

Discovering where the enchanted beetles had come from or *who* had sent them was going to be a whole different situation to sort out. But that was a problem for another day. I could only do so much at a time. Hopefully the coven would be able to perform a ritual or something and they would have answers for me.

I left Kizzi's, feeling hopeful now that I knew I could get rid of the beetles and rebuild my shop, one step at a time.

I burst back into Fiella's Finds, completely forgetting the vampire stranger I had left behind earlier. Once I had my mind set on an idea, I got tunnel vision and couldn't think about anything else.

His presence was so startling that I let out a humiliating squeal, my heart launching into my throat. I think I even jumped a few inches in the air.

"Woah there!" the vampire called out. "Just me! No need for theatrics."

I was lucky that the stranger wasn't a criminal looking to rob me of any trinkets that survived the avalanche.

I could not believe that he didn't just leave after I had abandoned him earlier. To my utter shock, it looked like he was actually... cleaning.

He wasn't cleaning very well, mind you. It looked like he was trying to sort through the mountain of wreckage and trinkets and form some sort of pile system. There was a pile of decimated wood chunks, a pile of items that looked only moderately damaged, and, to my disgust, there was also a growing pile of beetle carcasses. Gross.

He was touching those with his bare hands–how nasty. Who knew what sort of magical remnants would leech off them?

Hopefully Sookie hadn't eaten any. She was smarter than many folk but... she had her moments.

The vampire was tucked away behind some fallen roof boards, looking vaguely distressed and quite dusty.

"I didn't know where to start, and I was assigned here today, and there is clearly a lot of clean-up work needed, I figured I'd just..." He trailed off, gesturing aimlessly around the shop at the meager piles he had sorted.

My heart unexpectedly warmed a degree at the stranger's explanation.

"I can't really tell what's salvageable and what's not, a lot of these items are rather... unique." He didn't quite sound judgmental, he sounded more perplexed than anything.

I felt strangely touched by this stranger's actions. Even though I knew he just wanted to get his job done, the fact that he stayed to clean up when he could have easily left made me soften towards him. Just a bit. I still thought he was an asshole.

"That's pretty kind. Thank you, stranger," I said, fighting to keep my cheeks from warming. Was I actually *blushing* right now? What was I, a little? Embarrassing.

"I should've done this before but... Hello, my name is Fiella. And you are?"

The corner of his mouth lifted slightly. I couldn't tell if it was a grimace or a pitiful excuse for a smile. "Oh, you are ready for my name now? It's Redd."

Redd. That was a nice name. Strong.

"Well, thank you, Redd. My friend Kizzi is going to help me with a fumigation brew to kill the rest of these gods awful beetles, but it looks like I've got a lot of work ahead of me. Care to stick around? I can't pay you, but I can bless you with my presence and my lovely conversation."

He didn't laugh like I had expected him to. Like I hoped he would. *Tough crowd*. I'd make him crack one of these days–I was determined.

He waved a hand dismissively. "Mayor Tommins is paying me. I was assigned to help rebuild this shop, so I'm going to rebuild the shop. It needs to be cleaned first, though. This is clearly too big of a mess for one folk to manage," he stated matter-of-factly, though he appeared to be only half paying attention to the conversation. Offensive. He was too busy gazing around the room and looking a bit ill.

"Looks like we're in this together," I said. "At least for now."

I carefully made my way over to him, sticking my hand out for him to shake. His hand was warm and rough, his calluses scraping against my skin in a way that made a shiver run down my spine.

CHAPTER 10
Redd

"Looks like we're in this together. At least for now." I don't know why that thought made my stomach flip. It wasn't necessarily unpleasant, but it was interesting. Unsettling.

I didn't know what to expect from this woman. One moment she was screeching in my face, the next moment she was a blubbering mess, then she was a determined business owner, willing to do the hard work to save her shop. It was giving me whiplash.

I would have to keep my guard up—a woman like Fiella was bound to rip a man to shreds.

Fiella's hand was firmly grasped in mine, and a breeze flowed past her and jostled a few stray hairs on her head. Her scent barreled into me full force, making my body tense up involuntarily and my mouth water. Warmth and berries.

My throat flared red hot like a wildfire. I had never wished so strongly for a jar of thirst tonic in my life. I couldn't force my mouth to form any words in response.

I had a job to do, and I was determined to see it

through. If disasters were going to follow me wherever I went, I needed to resolve them quickly so I wouldn't drown in them.

The tense silence was interrupted by the loud grumbling of my stomach, which was echoed by a fierce, stabbing pain in my fangs. Gods, I was *starving* in more ways than one.

Fiella must've seen the discomfort on my face. She slowly pulled her hand from mine, and my palm felt cold. Empty.

"You know, you really should've taken one of the thirst tonics from Kizzi. I know how much of a pain in the ass it is to be thirsty. Vampire to vampire, the side effects are totally worth it, no matter how wacky they are. Kizzi's tonics are the best in the realm," she rambled. She must've been sensing the tension as much as I was.

I rolled my eyes. "Hells no. I've had my fair share of strangeness in the past few months. I can't afford any more surprises." That was an understatement.

If she was offended by my directness, she didn't let it show. She shrugged, stepping back. "Well, alrighty then, Mister Stranger. Suit yourself. But your growling stomach is starting to get on my nerves so go ahead and get yourself something to eat, I'll be fine here for the rest of the day."

"It's Redd," I grumbled. "We've been over this."

"I like *stranger* better. It's mysterious," she chirped, humor creeping into her voice.

For some reason, heat began creeping up my neck and into my cheeks. *Am I feverish? I must be.*

"If my growling stomach is such an inconvenience to you, then I'll get out of your blue hair." I grumbled. I was secretly relieved–I had forgotten to bring myself anything to eat today.

She merely hummed in response and turned to start sorting piles.

As I gathered my things, Fiella called over her shoulder. "See you tomorrow, I guess! Or whenever!"

I left the shop and headed towards the diner. I passed the same stone mailbox as before, and I idly glanced in its direction, my hands shoved deep in my cloak pockets as I walked along the cobblestone path.

I couldn't help but notice that the mailbox had a different sign on it this time, the paper a crisp white instead of a faded beige. My curiosity getting the best of me, I decided to take a closer look.

Sure enough, the sign was different.

This is for you. Yes, you.

I picked the sign up and flipped it over, only to notice a message on the back as well.

I mean it. You!

I glanced over my shoulder, looking for whatever prankster had left this sign. I didn't see any folk looking suspicious. There was a werewolf couple strolling hand in hand, a few humans meandering while laughing, and even a few orcs having a picnic with some faerie littles.

Grumbling under my breath about how ridiculous this was, I stuck my hand into the crumbling stone box. I had already earned enough bad luck; I couldn't afford to earn any more by ignoring the fates–even if this whole situation seemed fake and ridiculous.

To my utter surprise, my searching fingers found a folded piece of paper. This *had* to be a trick.

I pocketed the paper, deciding I'd rather read it in the comfort of my own cottage than be spied on by tricksters, and continued my way to the diner.

❧

The food at the diner was never disappointing. I'd even say, it might have been some of the best food I had ever eaten. The special tonight was a delicious beef and rice stew with freshly baked rolls on the side–everything steaming hot.

If I had to be in a room full of other people, I always preferred for food to be present. The scents of meats and spices helped drown out the smell of warm skin, of pumping hearts, of blood churning through veins. Instead, the nutmeg, chili, and sourdough were a soothing balm to my senses.

As I enjoyed my meal, I couldn't stop thinking about the letter that was burning a hole in my pocket. Or about the strange morning I had. Or about my family back home.

I slowly chewed on a bite of tender beef, thankful that the stew was gentle on my sore fangs. I reminded myself once again to search for some thirst tonic around town, to see if anyone but Kizzi could help me ease my miserable thirst.

When I finally made it back to my rental cottage on the edge of town, I let myself inside and immediately yanked out the letter, determined to unravel the mystery once and for all.

What I found was... peculiar. It was some sort of letter. The paper was more crumpled than folded, soaked in

64

spilled ink, and covered in scrawling script that I had to squint to make out.

I took a deep breath, smoothed my hair back from my face, plopped onto the overstuffed couch, and read.

Dear Mysterious Entity in the Mailbox,

Hello, I answered! I'm half convinced that this letter will just rot away in the mailbox, but just in case someone finds it, I sincerely hope you enjoy this glimpse at my thoughts, because I am not in a position to mess with the fates.

It's your lucky day I guess!!! But not mine.

Are you a ghost? Are you a spirit? Are you a folk? I simply must know. I am just a regular 'ol folk, but I would make a great ghost. I would love to haunt people. I bet nothing bad happens to ghosts, except for the dying part that makes you a ghost... I wonder if ghosts can just be born as ghosts. I need to ask someone about that.

Anyways. Hey ghost/spirit/folk, have you ever felt like screaming into the void until your voice gives out? That's how I'm feeling right now. I have had an absolutely TERRIBLE day. The worst day I have ever had. Or at least the second worst day. It's hard to rank shitty days, you know.

I'm worried that my life might be ruined. I know what you're thinking, "This person is so whiny and dramatic!" well, whoever you are, you might be right, but you must understand. My entire life has been destroyed today, and I don't know what I'm going to do.

Thank you for reading, mysterious mailbox spirit. (if you are actually reading and this letter isn't just going into the abyss...)

P.S. Zero alcohol went into the writing of this letter, by the way. None. Not a drop. Not even a few sips.

P.P.S. I wonder if anyone is actually going to read this.

I couldn't read the signature at the bottom–the sender was a complete mystery.

Gods be damned. Well, now I *had* to respond. This was too intriguing to pass up.

I pulled out my stack of parchment and my favorite ink and quill and set the letter aside so I could send a response of my own.

What was there to lose? Everything was already a mess anyways.

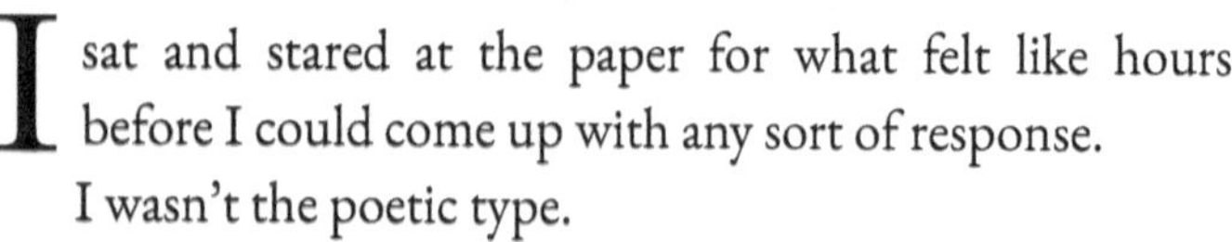

I sat and stared at the paper for what felt like hours before I could come up with any sort of response.
I wasn't the poetic type.

This is so stupid. I'm a grown man, grown men don't write letters to emotional strangers.

Ultimately, I decided that it didn't matter, since I was still somewhat convinced that this was all some elaborate prank.

But what if it wasn't a prank?

Eh, it was probably a prank.

Hello, Stranger.

I received your letter. Though I'm not sure when you wrote it, or who it was intended for, it has made its way into my hands.

I have many questions, but I'll save my ink for now.

I am not a ghost, nor am I a spirit. I am a regular folk, as you have said. I have never died, nor have I been to the afterlife. And I do not reside within any mailbox.

I am sorry about your day. If it helps, you are not alone. I have had days like that. And I assure you, it will pass. The lows don't last forever. You will rise again. Just get up tomorrow and keep going.

And do the same thing the next day.

Best,
Another Stranger

P.S. Alcohol, you say? Was it ale? Golden ale is my favorite.

I felt like an absolute idiot as I stared at the two letters in my hands. I was torn. Part of me wanted to crumple them both up, chuck them in the trash, and then act like this whole thing never happened. I was strangely embarrassed at having been roped into this odd predicament.

Another part of me was curious.

I sat for long minutes, my mind battling with itself.

Ultimately, the curiosity won out.

What do I have to lose?

Not allowing myself to dwell on the strangeness of the situation, I folded the parchment and left it on the corner of the table, promising myself that I would drop it in the mailbox on my next journey into town.

CHAPTER 11

Fiella

I couldn't shake the dark, gloomy cloud that followed me. My soul ached, throbbing incessantly, and I struggled to muster up any smiles for the friendly townsfolk of Moonvale. The corners of my mouth refused to lift.

After two days of intense, back-aching work at my shop, I decided that I needed a break.

I ate a quick lunch at the diner, grabbed a mid-day tea and pastry, and parked myself on my favorite bench in the park beside town square. Today, I had decided on a tart filled with strawberry jam (because it reminded me of blood, of course) and earl gray tea with mint leaves tossed on top.

I had tired myself out wrangling wreckage all morning, and my overworked muscles were burning. I needed some peace away from the annoying, grumpy vampire that had been dropping by my shop with a toolbag and a bad attitude.

Though I needed his help, I wasn't in the mood for his

company, and he didn't seem to be in the mood for mine either. We hardly spoke two words to each other.

It was for the best.

While munching on my delicious snack, my eye caught a slip of something white sticking out from under the bench. Was that... paper? I quickly scarfed down the last bite of tart and smacked my hands together to remove any lingering crumbs.

The paper was buried under some leaves, so I gently extracted it, brushed it off, and placed it in my lap. It looked like some sort of letter.

I considered putting the letter back and leaving it alone. It could have been left there on purpose for someone else. I looked around to see if anyone was watching me, if anyone seemed like they belonged to this letter.

None of the townsfolk paid me any mind. I made brief eye contact with a squirrel, but it scurried away after snatching up one of my wayward tart crumbs.

I sighed. I was too nosy to leave that treasure untouched, so of course I was going to read it. I couldn't help myself.

I glanced around one more time to be sure my snooping wouldn't be noticed before I quickly unfolded the paper.

Hello, Stranger.

I received your letter. Though I'm not sure when you wrote it, or who it was intended for, it has made its way into my hands.

I have many questions, but I'll save my ink for now.

I am not a ghost, nor am I a spirit. I am a regular folk, as you have said. I have never died, nor have I been to the afterlife. And I do not reside within any mailbox.

I am sorry about your day. If it helps, you are not alone. I have had days like that. And I assure you, it will pass. The lows don't last forever. You will rise again. Just get up tomorrow and keep going.

And do the same thing the next day.

Best,
Another Stranger

P.S. Alcohol, you say? Was it ale? Golden ale is my favorite.

What the fuck.

Well... Huh. I was dumbfounded.

I let the letter flutter to my lap as I scrubbed my eyes with my fists. I had dropped a letter in that old decrepit mailbox the other day, but I couldn't quite remember what

I had written. I vividly remembered writing something about ghosts, though. That line was a winner. Was it possible that this letter was somehow for me?

The thought seemed ridiculous.

But... It did seem to respond to my drunken rambling.

I didn't know how in the realms this letter found me, or how in the realms this stranger somehow received my letter and decided to respond. My mind was spinning.

This had to be the fates... right?

Strangely, just knowing that someone had read my worries and cared enough to respond lightened my heavy spirit, just a bit. It was amazing how much of a difference that small dose of companionship made. I never felt heard or understood by anyone other than Kizzi, but this stranger had read my rambling worries, and instead of simply tossing the letter into flame, they took the time to respond.

I had plenty of friends and neighbors, sure, but I kept it surface-level with pretty much everyone. If I let them peek under the hood of my thoughts, I was sure they would run screaming, so I kept most things to myself.

Maybe I didn't have to do that anymore.

I took a sip of my minty earl gray, feeling a bit lighter, and carefully folded the letter and tucked it into my pocket.

I caught myself feeling the beginnings of hope during my walk back to the shop.

Even knowing I had to see that annoying, rude vampire again wasn't enough to squash the kernel of light that had bloomed in my chest.

Aforementioned vampire was carefully lifting a massive stone bowl from the rubble when I strolled in the front door. I hardly paid him any mind–my thoughts still wrapped up in the mysterious letter. I heard the thud when he set it onto the exposed stone floor.

I plopped the letter, along with the other contents of my pockets onto my newly-designated worktable–pastry wrappers, a handful of clovers, a pinecone, and a tie for my hair. The table was more like a stool, a small square of wood supported by three legs, but it was a place to set my things and that was all that mattered.

I dove back into cleaning. Sookie would probably knock the clovers I had picked onto the floor, but I would just clean them up and pick more at the park tomorrow. One could never find too many good luck charms.

I don't even know if Redd noticed I was back–he was buried elbow-deep in wreckage–until his voice called out.

"You should really quit leaving the shop in the care of a stranger." He glanced at the hand-painted plates in his hand. "What if I was a thief who was after unnecessarily decorated plates?"

I crossed my arms, donned my most fearsome facial expression, and marched over to him. Well, march might not have been the right term because I had to climb over multiple piles on the way, but I gave it a strong effort.

I got into his space and glowered at him.

"I could take you down in an instant," I declared.

He set down the plates he was carrying and straightened to his full height. Gods damned, I was not used to anyone being able to tower over me. I kept forgetting I wasn't the tallest one in the room anymore.

"You think so, little vampire?"

He chuckled under his breath and turned around, mumbling something about feisty creatures.

How dare he! I lunged at his back, prepared to press my teeth into his jugular to prove my point that I was an intimidating woman who could take down *any* creature. I wasn't actually going to bite him, but I was definitely going to scare him.

He must've expected the move, because he whirled and snatched me by the shoulders, freezing me in place. Gods damn it, I thought I had him.

He held me still, just inches from his face. His breath brushed over me, smelling like peppermint and sugar, before it ceased entirely.

"Down, girl. Be good," he whispered. I shivered. I should've been infuriated by him speaking down to me like I was a wild animal but for some reason... It affected me differently.

After I remembered how to breathe, I yanked my shoulders from his grip and twirled in the opposite direction.

"I was trying to prove a point!" I said, flustered.

"And did you?" he answered drily.

"Um. Yes. Well. I was just trying to–I... I need to go next door and see if they have any extra brooms," I stammered. *I need to get out of here.*

I didn't wait for his response before hustling out the door.

Strangely, I felt no trepidation about leaving Redd alone in my shop once again. If he was going to take advantage of the situation, he surely would've done so by now.

CHAPTER 12
Fiella

"Sorry for barging in like this, Lunette—I needed some peace and quiet," I explained to my favorite neighbor as I wandered throughout her shop, grazing my fingers along the leaves of the plants lining the windowsills.

Lunette owned the plant shop next door, Lu's Blooms, and she was the best. The druid woman was a peaceful presence, always supportive and welcoming of my company. She was almost as tall as I was, so we bonded in ridiculous-height-solidarity. And she always smelled like cherries.

"No worries, Fi, you know you're welcome any time. Just don't touch that one!" She swatted my wandering fingers away from a particularly interesting looking plant. It had red leaves that looked almost spiky.

"Let me guess, it's poisonous?" I asked, taking a few steps away from the monstrous plant in case the air around it was toxic as well. "You idiot, you're going to get yourself in trouble again! You know you're supposed to keep things safe around here," I admonished.

Last year, Lunette got herself into a sticky situation

regarding a plant that induced extreme nausea. It was *not* pretty.

"Yeah, yeah, that only happened one time! This one is *clearly* labeled as "Do Not Touch" if you would have been paying attention," she explained as she flitted around the shop spraying her plants with enchanted water. She spared a moment to shoot me a sharp glare, but it didn't have any real heat behind it.

Lu's Blooms was like an oasis. The enchanted windows enhanced the sunlight streaming in, even during the freeze season, and kept the shop bright and warm.

I liked to come in here when I needed a breath of crispy, fresh air. Lunette's company was a plus as well.

"So..." Lunette said distractedly, untangling a persistent batch of vines. "What brings you over to my neck of the woods?"

I huffed out a deep breath and leaned my elbows onto the counter, bracing myself.

"I just tried to bite a stranger and now I'm hiding from him. Well, I guess he's not technically a stranger anymore, but still. I hardly know him."

Lunette dropped the vines she was working on, planted her hands on her hips, and turned to face me, finally giving me all of her attention. Unfortunately.

"Come again?" she asked. Her eyebrows were practically touching her hairline.

I explained, briefly, the situation I'd gotten myself into. From *the incident*, to Redd's involvement, to my attempt to pounce on him to prove myself able to protect my shop.

"Now Fi, why in the realms would you launch yourself

at him? What did you think was going to happen?!" she asked, exasperated.

"I don't know what came over me! I was seeing red! Literally! He implied that I was weak!"

"Well, you're going to have to face him again eventually," she muttered, trying but failing to hide her laughter. "What's your plan? Are you going to claim temporary insanity? Act like it never happened? Face it head on? Your options aren't great, but there are options."

"I was actually planning on diving into the river and never coming back, but I like your ideas better."

Lunette laughed full-on, tinkley and bright. Gods, she had the *best* laugh.

"You'll be fine. But you better come back later and keep me updated, you know I love hearing all the drama." She did–Lunette loved nothing more than a bit of juicy gossip.

I agreed to keep her in the loop. After chatting for a while longer and noticing that Lunette was subtly trying to get back to work, I decided to head back to my shop.

More time had passed than I thought, and the suns were sinking below the horizon. *Gods, how long was I there?* Time really passed differently in the oasis.

Blessedly, my shop was empty when I returned. No handsome vampires in sight. It was certainly for the best, because I had completely forgotten to grab a broom. My cover would have been blown.

I took a moment to sit and draft a letter before I locked up for the day, my hands shaking slightly. I couldn't quite identify the emotion that was seeping through my perpetual cloud of despair.

With a strange shiver of anticipation, I dropped the

folded paper into one of the crumbly mailboxes on my way home. I sure as hell wasn't going to bury it in the dirt where I had found the mysterious response earlier. I figured, if that letter found me, then surely this one could find its recipient as well.

My cheek might have twitched–the corner of my mouth making a pitiful attempt to lift into a smile. Though my soul was still withered, and my heart was still crushed from the devastating loss of my shop, I was finding new reasons to be hopeful.

CHAPTER 13
Redd

Gods, I was such an idiot.

I had clearly freaked Fiella out or made her uncomfortable enough that she couldn't stand to be in my presence anymore.

We already struggled to get along–I was a fool to make it even worse.

It wasn't my fault that my reflexes kicked in when the lovely vampire dove for my neck. I couldn't help but stop her. The urge to yank her head back and sink my fangs into her delicate flesh had been almost overwhelming, especially with my predator instincts on overdrive. It had taken the willpower of all the Old Gods combined to keep my mouth shut and away from her sweetly scented flesh.

Now *why* she dove for me was a mystery. This woman continued to beguile me. I couldn't even begin to understand her actions.

The confusion battled with the guilt I felt, both muddling my thoughts and making me feel... strange.

She fled faster than a water sprite escaping a fire, and

then she didn't come back, so I worked until my stomach started growling and then I made my leave. I wasn't going to hang around forever–I knew when my presence wasn't wanted anymore.

Now, I was sitting at the diner, picking at my plate of roasted wildbird and lemony potatoes, lost in my thoughts.

I wondered how everyone was doing back home in Sunhaven. They were surely doing better now than they were before I had left, as I had clearly brought the incessant bad luck here with me. Were my brothers managing the construction shop okay? Ollie was a hard worker, but he was very scatterbrained, and Wayde was the friendliest vamp there ever was but he got frustrated easily. They needed me around to level them out.

Was my Pa giving them a hard time? Was my Ma doing alright, was everyone being nice enough to her? I'd have to get a letter to them. They had sent me a few brief missives that I had received from Mayor Tommins, but they were mainly inquiring on when I'd be back without giving me much information.

I was brought back to reality when a hand landed on my shoulder.

I shrugged it off before turning around, fighting off the shiver of discomfort that threatened to roll down my spine. I didn't appreciate being touched without warning.

Mayor Tommins was standing behind me with a plate in his hand. "Care if I sit?" he asked, already pulling out the chair next to me. I wasn't sure why he even bothered asking. I held in a sigh.

"Sure, boss, go ahead."

Mayor Tommins plopped down with a huff, taking a

bite of roasted potatoes and a sip of dark ale before speaking again. There were plenty of open tables in the diner and I tried not to be irritated that he had chosen to sit by me. Some folk were just friendlier than others. Some folk also weren't great at reading a room.

"So, Mr. Ivyhurst, I'm sorry to say it, but I've got another job for you." He didn't seem very sorry, heartily scooping forkfuls of meat into his sharp-toothed mouth.

I once again held back a sigh. Of course he had another job for me. The tasks this town needed help with were never-ending. *At least I've got some job security here.* At this rate, I was going to have a mountain of silvers in my coffers by the end of the year.

Guilt tickled at the back of my mind. If the bad luck had somehow followed me here from Sunhaven, then I was the reason so many things around town needed fixing.

Maybe I should just camp out alone in the Barren Lands until this string of disasters ends. At least nobody else will be impacted if I'm on my own.

I tucked the idea away to consider more thoroughly later. I didn't have any proof yet that the tragedies were my fault. The problem was–I had no idea *how* I could possibly find proof. I hoped to the Old Gods that this giant mess would just clear itself up sooner rather than later. Magic wasn't endless, after all. And curses couldn't last forever.

I snapped back to the conversation when Mayor Tommins rhythmically tapped his fingers on the table. "I haven't finished up at Fiella's yet–it's taking longer than we expected," I explained. "There was a *lot* of cleanup needed."

"I'm sure Miss Elmwick can handle some of the

cleanup on her own. She is a very capable woman," he stated dismissively.

"Sure, sure." I didn't know what else to say to that. I knew very well how capable she was—she had been an absolute workhorse in the hours I had spent in her company.

"I need you to head over to the Widowlyns' farm on the north edge of the Greenwood Forest tomorrow. They've got a broken gate, and we can't afford to have livestock running through the town. You can get back to Fiella's disaster later—this one is urgent and should be fairly quick."

Every task seemed quite urgent, but I kept that unhelpful thought to myself. Tommins explained the details, finished up his meal, and then headed on his way. The gryphon sure could eat *fast*. It was impressive, honestly. I stared down at my half-eaten meal. The lemony roasted potatoes didn't seem quite as enticing anymore, though the crispy things had been delicious. I sighed and took another bite.

After I finished my meal, I ordered another ale along with a slice of berry pie. When the server slid the plate to me across the counter, I noticed a white corner sticking out from underneath.

What I had first thought was a napkin was really paper. Was that supposed to be there?

I tried to flag down the server, but he was already helping other customers, and he just looked confused at what I was trying to ask.

Fuck it. I picked up the letter and immediately recognized the handwriting, though it was much neater this time, and I could read it without squinting.

I couldn't prevent the smile that tugged on the corner of my mouth. Maybe today was looking up after all.

At the back of my mind, I worried that this was still some sort of prank, but I brushed that aside for now.

The letter-writer had responded.

I didn't put much thought into how it had ended up tucked under my pie plate at the diner.

Another Stranger?

I was pleased to receive your letter. I was fairly certain I wouldn't receive anything in response to that mess I sent before. Sorry about that, by the way. Not my finest work.

Am I to assume I am the first stranger, if you are "another"? Fine, at least I am the first. If you prefer to keep your identity a secret, I'll respect it. I like your style, I have always loved a good mystery. I shall call you Stranger 2.

Questions, you say? Ask away. Your response found me quickly, so I'm hoping this one finds you quickly as well.

I have questions of my own. Are you a witch of some sort? Is that how your letters have made their way to me? And why me? Have we met before? I'd assume so, if you're going to go through the effort of casting a spell, or paying someone else silvers to do it...

I must thank you for your words, and for your response. You have no idea how much I needed a kind soul, an encouraging word. So, this is me saying thank you.

Now, if this message somehow finds you again, though I have an inkling the fates will make it so,

I hope your days are peaceful and your fortune is better than mine is right now.

Be well,
Stranger 1

P.S. It was certainly not ale. Yuck. That's disgusting. I prefer ANY other beverage.

"Whatcha got there? Message from family?" the server asked.

I startled at the sound of his voice, quickly folding the letter back up and shoving it in my trouser pocket. I didn't know his name, and I didn't particularly care to learn it. He was polite enough, and that was plenty.

"Sure, something like that," I responded. "Anyways, thanks, for–" I gestured at the now-empty bowl in front of me. "–all this". I stood and placed a coin on the table.

I glanced around the diner to see if anyone had paid particular attention to me reading the letter, or for someone to be stifling laughter at having fooled me. I didn't see anything except for folk eating normally.

Shaking my head in exasperation, I hurried out of the diner.

~

From that point forward, the letter exchange continued.

Stranger One,

Your letter has found me once again. I must say, this correspondence has been surprising. Not unpleasant but... unexpected.

But not bad.

No, I am not a witch. I am not a magic user of any kind. Am I to assume you are a witch, then? It is rather strange how our letters have managed to be delivered back and forth. That will remain a mystery, unless you have some sort of explanation. I'm afraid I have no answers.

I am glad that my words were able to bring you a small amount of comfort. I've been bringing the folk around me nothing but pain and suffering lately, so it is a nice change of pace.

All the best,
Two

P.S. It is blasphemy that you think ale is disgusting. I can only assume that you have an underdeveloped palate.

Two,

If you are not the magical force behind our correspondence, It seems that the fates have pulled us together.

I'm certainly not complaining. I don't have the silvers to spare to send letters, so this is lovely. (I truly hope you are not spending silvers on this, or I will feel a bit stupid).

No offense, but I think you are a liar. There is no way that you bring nothing but pain and suffering to those around you. You offered kindness to a stranger you had never met, so that doesn't add up.

Do you have a family, Two? I do, sure, but they aren't around much anymore. If ever. I suppose my neighbors have become my makeshift family. I would love to hear about yours. Hopefully it is full, and loving, and wonderful.

Sending good vibes,
One

P.S. My palate is perfectly refined, thank you. Just because I prefer the taste of herbs and sugar over the taste of piss doesn't make me any less of a folk.

Sometimes, days passed, but the letters always turned up eventually.

Dear One,

You think I am a liar? After only two letters? Wow, you are quick to judge.

I won't hold it against you.

I have not spent any silvers, don't worry about that. I would, though, if I had to. It seems an outside force is keeping our correspondence going. Perhaps it is the fates. I am not going to complain about that either.

I do have a family. I miss them very much. I am not with them now, due to unfortunate circumstances, but I hope to return to them some time in the near future. I have recently moved away from them.

They are loud, and rambunctious, and annoying, but they are the best folk I know.

Where has your family gone, if that is alright to ask? Family doesn't have to be blood related, I'm sure your neighbors are a full, loving, wonderful family.

> I think I received some of those good vibes you
> sent.
> So I'm sending them back.
> Two

P.S. If you think that ale tastes like piss, then

my opinion stands that your palate has a lot of work to do. It's an acquired taste. Sugar water is for littles.

Two,

I'd say I'm a pretty good judge of character. If folk show you who you are, I think you should keep your eyes open and believe them.

To me, you seem like a good folk. So I am deciding that you are a good folk. And if your family is loud, rambunctious, AND annoying, they sound like they would be some of the best as well. I am glad that you have them.

I will admit, I've started to look forward to your letters. I find myself looking for them everywhere, searching for glimpses of paper wherever I go.

They aren't always in the mailbox, isn't that strange? The fates are mysterious, I guess.

Thank you,
One

P.S. I've upgraded to nicer paper, can you tell? I hope you appreciate it. I figured that if we are going to continue this, I might as well use some actual parchment instead of the crinkled stuff I was finding around my cottage.

Dear One,

I've caught myself looking forward to your letters as well. You are not alone in that.

When days are hard and my body is aching from my work, I find my mind wandering to when your next letter will find me. It is a strange sort of comfort. A distraction.

I find them in the mailboxes sometimes, but I find them in mysterious places as well. They even end up inside my cottage, isn't that ~~alarming~~ strange?

How have your days been faring, One? You were in a bad situation when you wrote your first letter. Have things gotten any better? I hope they have.

Yours,
Two

P.S. The new parchment is nice. But I remember you mentioning that you didn't have many silvers, so you should stop buying it. Don't waste silvers just to send me a letter, the old crinkly stuff is perfectly legible.

CHAPTER 14
Fiella

"Hey, beautiful bitches!"

I glanced up from my pile of broken teacups to see Kizzi entering the shop with a very suspicious looking cauldron in her arms. I was afraid the steaming liquid was going to slosh all over her front.

Red smoke wafted from the cauldron and crept across the floor. It smelled like maple syrup, something spicy, and... petrichor? Weird.

Redd, surprisingly, hardly reacted to Kizzi's dramatic entrance. This vampire was hard to rattle.

We had been working together on and off for more than two weeks now, and I learned that nothing seemed to faze him. It was *so* annoying.

"Please tell me that's for the beetles and not something you want me to drink," I mumbled. I still got queasy when I thought about the last time Kizzi made me sample something from her cauldron.

Charcoal, lemongrass, fish guts, and gods knew what else. And she didn't even warn *me first. Asshole.*

94

"It issssssss!" she sang, twirling alarmingly with the cauldron lifted above her head. She was definitely going to make a mess.

Redd snatched the cauldron from her before any disasters could strike. Smart man.

Kizzi explained to us the extremely dramatic process of activating the potion, which would involve an embarrassing dancing-and-chanting situation.

I didn't know *much* about magic, but I was pretty sure she was just messing with us at this point.

"Sookie!" I yelled out to the cat. She might not have belonged to me, but she *always* came when I called. My girl.

She meandered into the room, yawning. She had clearly just been napping somewhere.

I scooped her up and tossed her outside, quietly explaining to her that she did *not* want to witness this. She didn't seem to mind much. I was pretty sure she was smarter than most folk I knew, and I didn't want her judgmental ass around to mock me for what was about to happen.

"Okay, now I'm ready," I said tentatively. I twisted my hair up into a tight knot, wanting to keep it out of my face for whatever was going to occur here.

"Alright, I'm the boss. Here's what's about to happen," Kizzi proclaimed. She proceeded to explain the steps of the ritual, listing them off on her fingers as she did so.

1. We needed to burn sage, and then place crystals and herb bundles evenly around the whole shop.

2. We needed to join hands and skip around in a circle fifty times, to begin the energy cyclone.
3. We needed to all (unfortunately) drink a ladle of the potion.
4. The big finale, we needed to boil the potion until it reduced and burnt to ashes, while "singing the clarity song", whatever that was.

If we did everything correctly, the remaining magical beetles would drop dead, and we'd be able to sweep them away and act like they never existed in the first place. At least, that was my plan. I shivered just thinking about it. *Gods, I hate bugs.*

I still didn't know where they came from or who had sent them here, but that was a problem for future Fiella. Right now, I just wanted them gone. It had been a nightmare trying to squish the insects and shoo them away while cleaning up the mess they had caused. They slowed the process down immensely.

Redd was grumbling under his breath, something that sounded like "... got to be fucking kidding me..." but I chose to ignore him. He could grow up and prance around the room with us like a real man.

"Okay, whatever, let's get this over with."

"Great! This is going to be fun!" Kizzi shouted, clapping her hands and bouncing on her toes like this was the most exciting event in the realms.

She was lucky I loved her, because sometimes she was *annoying*.

~

"No, not there, *there!*" Kizzi called for what felt like the hundredth time. Redd was not very good at strategic crystal placing, apparently. I had to stifle my laughs.

Redd grumbled under his breath but moved the crystal to the correct location. It had taken us *way* longer than it should have to set everything out properly.

"Finally! Alright that feels good, I can sense the magic aligning. Now we need to whip it up and get this thing rolling," Kizzi stated, grabbing my hand and yanking me to the cauldron in the center of the room.

Redd reluctantly joined us, looking like he'd rather be doing literally anything else. He grasped our hands and completed the circle.

His hand was warm, strong, and calloused and his grip sent a shiver of awareness through me.

Gods damned, I was embarrassingly touch starved. I bet a full-blown hug would knock me off my feet.

Looking like fools, we spun and spun and spun until I was sure I was either going to fall over or be sick. Both options were not ideal. Redd was looking a little green in the face so at least I wasn't the only one.

Kizzi looked green too, but that was nothing unusual for her. She usually fluctuated between shades of brown and jade. Maybe she was a bit greener? She was smiling and giggling like a little, though, so she was probably feeling perfectly fine.

Before I could make a new mess on the (already very messy) floor and embarrass myself any further, Kizzi declared that the magical energy had been sufficiently whipped and we could now proceed with the rest of the spell.

I didn't know what whipped magic felt like, but the hair on my arms was raised a bit. And there was a slight knot in my stomach, but that could've just been indigestion. Or a lingering hangover.

We all collapsed onto the floor, our brains spinning. Thank the gods Sookie was gone–she probably would've been internally laughing her cat ass off at the spectacle. It took us a few minutes to be stable enough to pass around the cauldron ladle.

This concoction wasn't as dreadful as the last one I had tried, but it certainly wasn't pleasant. Sea water, maple syrup, dried grass, sweet cream, and... was that fur? I tried not to think about it too hard as I held my breath and swallowed the concerningly textured mouthful.

I needed to stop letting Kizzi feed me things. She had a bad track record.

My still-tender stomach heaved, but I managed to keep the liquid down. Redd actually gagged once. Softie. I barely held myself back from making any rude comments. I was surprised that the surly vampire had stayed for the ritual, as he could have easily made an excuse and left, but Kizzi did tend to have that effect on people. It was Kizzi's realm, and we were all just living in it.

It was inspirational, honestly.

Stomach full of a mysterious magical liquid, I was beginning to feel the magic in the shop more acutely. The magic of the potion was moth wings fluttering in my stomach, the whipped natural magic was gentle breezes kissing my skin, and the lingering magic of the beetles was pins and needles in my legs and acidic burning in my nostrils.

It must be strange to be a witch, to constantly be so in touch with the lingering magic in the world. The magic must have been overwhelming ages ago, when the Old Gods' magic was still flooding the realm. Witches weren't the only creatures able to connect with magic–sprites, elves, faeries, and other folk could as well, but witches and wizards were the best at it.

"Time for the final stages. We've got to boil and burn this stuff and repeat this tune," Kizzi stated. "Fi and I will take the high notes, tough guy over there is going to take the low notes. Let's harmonize."

"Is that necessary?" Redd asked uncertainly. "Back home the witches usually just chant their spells. In normal speaking voices."

"Boo, you guys are no fun," Kizzi complained. "Whatever."

Kizzi placed the cauldron on a hot plate and tossed a lit match on top. The liquid, somehow, caught fire.

We sang (or chanted, because Redd was lame) the verse for what felt like hours but was probably more only like thirty minutes. The stuff burned down pretty quickly.

I was exhausted, and my throat was hurting. I couldn't tell if that was from my lovely singing or if thirst was creeping back up on me. Probably a mixture of both.

Redd was a surprisingly good sport about the whole situation, all things considered. He complained under his breath the whole time, but he stayed and helped, and that was what mattered. I developed a crumb or two of respect for the vampire. Not quite admiration, but definitely respect.

"So, Kiz, did it work?" I finally asked. I was so tired and overwhelmed with magic that I could barely keep track of my own two feet. The shop was filled with hazy smoke, and I had to resist the urge to cough.

"Of course it worked! It's me!" Kizzi responded, cocky as always. "Can't you smell the difference?"

"Honestly, I think my nose hairs are singed off. I won't be able to smell anything for weeks." I responded. Redd grunted in agreement.

"Well, take my word for it then. It smells *much* better. And look, those pesky beasts are already dropping."

Sure enough, she was right. Glancing around, mixed in with the mess, the beetles were no longer moving. There were *hundreds* of them. Yuck. They must've come out from their hiding spots during the ritual. I was glad I didn't realize the vast number of them before, because that surely would have given me a panic attack.

"My savior!" I proclaimed dramatically, throwing my arms around Kizzi's shoulders. She shoved me off immediately.

"Yeah yeah, I'm the best, I already know it. You owe me one, bitch!"

"I owe you more than one," I stated, feeling more serious than before. I didn't try to hug her again, but I did place my hand on her shoulder. "I owe you everything. You know how much this shop means to me. I mean it–thank you. I'm lucky to have a friend like you in my life."

"Oh, come on, don't get sappy on me now!" She patted my hand that was on her shoulder but returned my seriousness. "I know. And you know I always have your back. We're in this together. To the moons."

"To the suns." I smiled.

"Now let's get out of here! It's going to take forever for the fumes to dissipate and we've done enough work for one day."

"Cheers to that!"

We linked elbows and walked out of the shop.

"Redd, you coming?" Kizzi asked.

I'd almost forgotten he was there. "No, you guys go ahead, I've had enough excitement for one day." He stated.

I shrugged, moving on. Like I said, he was lame. Kizzi and I headed to the diner.

CHAPTER 15
Fiella

"Shut up!" Kizzi exclaimed. "Those old dusty mailboxes that are all over the place? No way."

Over bowls of veggie soup and rice, I had explained to Kizzi what had happened with the mailboxes and my new mysterious penpal.

"I know it sounds crazy but it's true! I don't have the letters here to prove it but I swear!" I had the letters tucked away under my counter in my shop, along with the fancy new stack of paper I had purchased from the market.

"I had always sensed some remnants of magic around those things, but I figured it was just residual crumbs from back in the day. You know those things used to instantly transport anything inside of them to any other mailbox in the realm? *Anywhere*. Instantly." She had a dreamy look on her face, clearly swooning over the idea of that vast amount of magic.

I snapped my fingers in front of her face. "Snap out of it, you're drooling."

"Sorry, sorry, but can you *imagine* that much magic?"

She shoved a bite of carrot into her mouth and chewed distractedly.

"I've read about it in a few books, it seemed like they took it for granted back then. Did you know every single building in the realm had enchanted lighting? And it wasn't outrageously expensive? They had these lines that ran between every place that carried the magical currents. Must've been nice." I was only a bit jealous. That was a lie—I was seething with jealousy. I couldn't even afford one enchanted sconce for my cottage right now.

"Right! Ugh. If they ever develop a way to travel back in time, we should go back and knock some sense into those fools," she mused. "So, about this mysterious letter writer—do you know who it is?"

I sighed. "No! I don't have a clue. I hardly know anything about them. We sort of skipped over all the introductory stuff and dove straight into soul searching. It feels like it's too late now to ask any of those questions—it would ruin everything."

She seemed to contemplate this. "I see where you're coming from. So, you don't even know if they're here in Moonvale? It seems like the letters are from here in town, but I suppose they could technically be coming from anywhere."

I took a sip of mint water. "Nope! Not a clue. I don't really know any identifying information about them, now that I think about it. They've moved away from their family, so they're feeling a bit lonely. They didn't mention where they moved to. Or from."

"Nobody can replace me as a best friend. You better not even try," she grumbled.

"I would never! You know you're my person. But a little extra companionship couldn't hurt."

"Is there a flirty vibe there? Do you think they're handsome? Or pretty? Or cute or whatever? Do they give off good-looking vibes?"

I laughed. "I don't know! Their handwriting is great, and their brain sure is sexy. If the outside matches the inside, I'm sure they're as hot as Hell's Realm."

"You should try to figure out who they are!" Kizzi insisted.

I let the thought sink in. What if I could meet my penpal in real life? It almost seemed too good to be true, but just for a moment, I let myself daydream about it.

And then I snapped myself back to reality and accepted that the thought was nonsense, and having a long distance penpal was a perfectly fine thing to do. I didn't want to risk ruining one of the only good things I had going on in my life.

"Enough about me. What's up with you?" I asked.

"Ugh, finally!" Kizzi exclaimed dramatically. "I've been waiting for you to ask!"

I rolled my eyes at her, gesturing with my hand for her to continue.

"Well, actually, things have been pretty tense around the apothecary." She stopped herself, glancing guiltily in my direction. "Well, not nearly as bad as your situation, of course."

I interrupted, "Kiz, it's fine. Just because I'm going through something doesn't mean that you aren't allowed to have your own struggles too." I reached over and patted her on the shoulder. "It's not a competition. Now please, tell me all about it."

She smiled tentatively, letting out a breath so deep it made her shoulders sink. "You're right, you're right. I know. I just don't want to overstep."

"We're way past that and you know it."

"You're right, once again. Gods damn, when did you get so wise?"

We both chuckled at that one.

"So, you know how those sprites have been messing with me for a while? Well, of course you know, nevermind." She tossed a glance at my blue tresses that had remained bright as I slowly worked through my tainted jar of thirst tonic. "Well, I've been trying to get on top of it, but they seem to be one step ahead of me. Every time! This morning, the joint-pain-relieving tea leaves I spelled for Ani, you know the old coven leader, were replaced with those *relaxation* herbs, and mirthroot. You should've seen it!"

That was a mental image I wouldn't be forgetting any time soon. I would pay so many silvers to witness that.

My jaw dropped open. "You're kidding! Gods, I can't believe I missed that!"

She nodded sagely. "It was hilarious, and it took all of my willpower to stay professional and stop myself from laughing. Hardest thing I've ever done. But seriously, it's getting worse. I'm going to have to try something stronger."

We discussed strategies for her situation as we finished our meal.

I often thought about how lucky I was to have crossed paths with Kizzi. We had been friends for years, since we were littles, and we had been joined at the hip for as long as

I could remember. I truly would lose my sanity without her, and I was pretty sure she felt the same about me.

"Ew, don't smile at me all nostalgic like that, it's creepy," Kizzi said as she tossed a chunk of bread at my face.

I laughed, shaking my head as I snapped back to the conversation.

CHAPTER 16
Redd

My mind was still reeling from the ridiculous ritual at Fiella's shop.

I had been around plenty of rituals and witches in my life, but Kizzi's style was something else entirely. At least it had worked–I had to give her credit for that.

I had wandered back to my cottage after the event, but when my stomach started growling and my throat started pulsing along with my heartbeat, I begrudgingly made my way back to town to find something to eat.

It had been entirely too many days since I had dosed myself with thirst tonic, and even with the increased animal blood I had been drinking, I was suffering.

When I entered the diner, my eyes were drawn to bouncy blue hair at a table off to the side. Fiella and Kizzi were so absorbed in their own conversation that they didn't notice anyone else around them.

I made sure to stay out of their lines of sight. I had endured enough for one day and I was drained. And also vaguely humiliated. Skipping in circles could do that to a man.

There were so many bodies in one room—so many hearts pumping hot, delicious-smelling blood through veins and arteries. So many necks vulnerable to being bitten. I took a deep breath through my mouth, cooling the fire in my throat and giving my nose a reprieve from the onslaught. I tried to focus on the food smells, but the cooking vegetables weren't as potent as the smell of meat, so they didn't drown out the blood smells as well.

Gods, this is miserable.

I grabbed my bowl of rice and soup to go, promising to bring the dishes back tomorrow, and made my way back to my cottage where I could enjoy my meal in private.

I didn't have family to talk to here in Moonvale like I had back at home, so there wasn't much here to entertain myself with besides books. I decided now was as good a time as any to write a letter to my parents back in Sunhaven.

Weeks had passed, and I was sure they were worried about me. I hadn't been communicating as well as I should have been.

I briefly mentioned that I was doing just fine here, and that they didn't have to worry about me. I left out any mentions of the massive workload I was juggling here, and that this town seemed to be a disaster. I left out anything that could possibly make them worry or wonder if I had made a mistake in coming here. I didn't want to cause my Ma any unnecessary stress.

I asked how everyone was doing—Ollie and Wayde, my parents, the shop, the neighbors, *everyone*. I asked how the weather was, because it was dreadfully cold here. Bone chilling, really. I missed the heat almost as much as I missed my Ma's homemade blood and beef stew.

I asked if the bad luck had dissipated when I left.

After I finished the letter, which was much longer than I had anticipated, I headed back into town to ask Mayor Tommins about how Moonvale handled letter delivery. I was sure they had some sort of critter or carrier system here, and since the suns were still above the horizon, there should have been plenty of time to figure it out. I had received a few letters, so surely there was a way to send them to other towns as well.

I wished it was as easy as it had been with my penpal– those letters simply delivered themselves. My insides warmed slightly at the reminder.

It turned out that Moonvale had a handful of carrier parrots available, and I paid to have one dispatch my message. That method was much cheaper than having the letter instantly sent via magical spell, which would cost me a week's worth of silvers. I would rather save my coins than waste them on convenience.

The town slowed down as the suns sank past their peak. Folk slunk away to their homes– the critters curled into their nests, and the night insects began their chirping.

It was peaceful. I was used to noise and bustle back home in Sunhaven, and the serenity was a nice change of pace. The buildings here were so spread apart, none of them sharing walls and each looking vastly different.

My favorite part about Moonvale was the Greenwood Forest it was nestled beside. The trees were massive– reaching their limbs outwards like fingers, searching for something to brush up against. The air smelled alive, like dirt and fresh blades of grass.

I stuck my hand into a mailbox as I passed by, my fingers encountering crisp, expensive parchment.

I smiled, my mood lifting instantly as I tucked the letter into my cloak.

Ground-dwelling plants swallowed up the cobblestones as I trudged back toward my cottage.

My friend Two,

I hope it is okay if I start calling you my friend.

Things have been slowly looking up. The days are hard, and I often find myself sinking back into the hold of self-pity, but I am trying to stay positive.

I'm telling myself things can only get better from here.
They are getting better. Bit by bit.

And how are you, friend? Has your body been holding up through those long days you told me about? I hear they make tonics for that sort of thing, you should look into finding some. I don't like hearing that you are in pain.

Your friend,
One

P.S. I appreciate your concern about my stash of silvers, but this was a worthwhile investment.

The suns had not yet set, but I was exhausted. I collapsed into bed with a mystery book so I could read until I fell asleep. A good story would keep my mind occupied and prevent it from wandering.

Mayor Tommins had, unsurprisingly, given me another work assignment for tomorrow. I would be tackling that bright and early.

I'd get back to Fiella's shop whenever I had the time.

She would be fine as she always was. She was tough, even if she did cry sometimes. That didn't erase her strength.

I shook my head to scatter my thoughts, as they had begun to settle on Fiella. I didn't want to think about the infuriatingly lovely vampire any more than I already did. Her scent haunted me every time I worked beside her; I didn't want the idea of her to haunt me in her absence as well.

The next few days blurred together into an endless cycle of working, sleeping when my body gave out on me, and eating when I could spare a moment for it. I was so busy that I hardly had time to think, let alone do anything else. It seemed that every single folk in Moonvale needed assistance in one way or another. If there wasn't something to rebuild, there was a mess to help clean, or heavy things that needed moving, or cats that needed help getting down from trees. Not many folk here were tall enough to reach, apparently.

I was guzzling down animal blood beverages every chance I could, but without the sense-dulling properties of a thirst tonic to sooth the flames in my throat and the aching in my fangs, they hardly took the edge off.

I had to get some thirst tonic in my system soon or I would be in unbearable misery, worse than I already was. I was hanging on by a thread.

I'd stopped by Kizzi's yesterday when I had a moment's reprieve, but the witch had seemed so busy and flustered and she hadn't had the chance to mix up any more tonics. If she didn't brew any soon, I would have to travel somewhere else. I was getting desperate.

I was becoming extremely familiar with this town, as my work had taken me down every single street. I felt like a bee, buzzing from flower to flower on an endless cycle. Except I wasn't even serving a queen, I was serving Mayor Tommins and the mess that was Moonvale.

A few days had passed before I heard back from my family. The letter left a sour taste in my mouth and an uneasy feeling in the pit of my stomach. My Ma had ignored most of my questions and instead just asked again about when I would be home. That wasn't like her. I had immediately penned another response, but I couldn't help but worry about them in the meantime.

Hadn't things gotten better once I left? Surely, they had–everyone would certainly be doing better now.

Right?

A few months ago, bad things had started to happen in Sunhaven. Tools would go missing. Orders would get misplaced. Wood beams would splinter in half without explanation. Then bigger things started happening–a fire at the bakery I frequented, my friend Brale falling ill immediately after seeing me, and my family's carriage breaking down. Somehow, it all seemed to be connected to me. I convinced myself that I was the cause. That I was cursed. That I was bad luck.

So I fled. To save myself, and to spare everyone else.

I wouldn't be able to get my family off my mind until I heard back again–until they reassured me that everything was fine. I had a bad feeling that something big was going on, but I wasn't sure what. And I didn't know how to fix it without admitting to everyone that I was somehow at fault.

CHAPTER 17
Fiella

The next letter found me in an unexpected place—tucked under the water jug I used to water my plants.

Dear One,

You can call me whatever you'd like.

I am glad that things have been getting better for you. Very glad, actually. You deserve peace and prosperity. Happiness, too.

I am holding up. I am tired, always, but the work I do is important. I'm needed here, and it is a good feeling to be needed.

I am conflicted, though. I don't belong here.

I have been trying to avoid tonics recently, but I might consider it. I'm used to aches and pains, though. It comes with the territory.

Your friend,
Two

I placed the letter back where I found it, making a mental note to respond later, when I wasn't quite so busy.

Days went by without any appearances from Redd, and I hated to admit that a small part of me missed his presence. He was grumbly and annoying, but he was strong. And having an extra set of hands around made the cleanup effort go by so much faster.

I had spent an entire five days just cleaning up beetle carcasses from every single nook and cranny in the shop. It was almost as though they were multiplying—every time I felt I had made progress, more appeared. I purposely avoided counting them (because I was protecting my fragile sanity) but there were *a lot*.

Sookie was around to keep me company, and she even brought in a few of the other local cats with her from time to time. She always seemed to be hanging around with a huge orange tabby and a smaller striped cat. I could just tell they were the cool cats in town, they were better than all the other cats. It was possible that I was biased.

I had left my windows and doors open for as long as I could stand it, but the cold air was relentless. I could've sworn it was getting colder instead of warmer, but that must've been my imagination. According to the calendar, Moonvale was rapidly approaching the mild season, so warm sunny days were only a few weeks away.

For today, though, it was gods damned *frigid*.

I was convinced that the horrendous smell of the beetles combined with the fumigation brew was still lingering in the shop, but I could sacrifice my sense of smell to spare myself from the relentless shivering.

I eventually sealed up the sack of beetles I'd been collecting and decided to pay a visit to my neighbors to see how they were faring. Mayor Tommins hadn't been bluffing when he had mentioned that I wasn't the only one with issues–the problem seemed to be fairly widespread.

I knew how hard it was to ask for help, even when it was needed.

"Hey, Lune!" I called out as I pushed open the door to the plant shop. Lunette hadn't been struck by tragedy, as far as I could tell. She was one of the lucky ones. I wondered what kind of good luck charm she was carrying around with her.

"Coming! One sec! Just hang on and don't touch anything!" I heard her voice call from one of the back rooms. I busied myself by admiring her new display of decorative mosses. There was an especially eye-catching moss patch that seemed to reflect light in a dazzling, glittery display.

Lunette had a knack for tracking down the most gorgeous plants in the whole realm. I had spent a lot of my silvers here, buying plants for my cottage and my shop. I couldn't help it, I was obsessed! Even if I killed them from time to time, Lunette never judged me when I came back searching for replacements. I had developed a decently green thumb over the years. Not entirely green, but certainly green-tinted.

A few minutes later, Lunette appeared from the back room, covered in dirt, her eyes rapidly darting around the shop.

"What's up with you? You look like you just rolled around in a mud puddle. Everything okay?" I asked, moving to the next table to admire a dazzling pothos vine that had pink spots. I made a mental note to get myself one of those too, once my shop was back in order.

She grabbed a towel from a nearby table and started wiping off her hands. "Oh, everything's fine, just got a shipment that wasn't packaged well, and things became a mess. I've got it handled," she answered hurriedly.

"Anything I can help with?" I asked. Lunette was usually pretty chill–it was unsettling to see her looking so rattled.

"No, no. Just an accident. Nothing I can't handle," she

explained while wrangling her orange hair back into its twist.

"Was it more of those toxic plants?" I asked hesitantly.

She looked at me guiltily but didn't answer.

"Lunette! You better be filling out all the paperwork for those. I'm going to be pissed if you get thrown into the mayor's dungeon and leave me neighborless!"

"They're not all toxic! Only a few of them. Okay fine, most of them. But I won't get in trouble this time, I'm certain. Kizzi and Mayor Tommins requested them–apparently, they are in need of some spotted thorn ivy plants for one of Kizzi's potions. I didn't ask too many questions."

There was a lot of information to unpack there. If Mayor Tommins was backing the plant imports, then they couldn't be *that* dangerous, I assumed.

Lunette refused to let me help her with cleanup. Something about how I never paid enough attention and would probably touch my face after touching something poisonous... Whatever! To each their own!

We chatted for a bit, until I began to sense that she was just humoring me to be polite and her mind was stuck elsewhere. I knew how to read a room.

I left, feeling vaguely concerned and more than a little confused. *That was strange.*

I decided to check on Kizzi instead–maybe she would need some sort of help. Fates knew she had helped me so much recently; it was about time I returned the favor.

~

Kizzi's shop was a mess. But that was nothing new. Just looking around made my heart rate increase in secondhand anxiety. My own mess was something I could handle. Anyone else's mess was panic inducing.

Kizzi had been having strange shop mishaps for as long as she had been running the shop, so she was used to dealing with minor tragedies. Like my blue hair, that I was becoming strangely attached to.

Whether things had gotten worse lately, though, well that was what I had come to find out.

The racks of bottles and test tubes and jars were disorganized, the sachets of herbs and flowers were randomly piled into baskets, and cauldrons of mysterious coagulated liquid were haphazardly placed on counters.

Honestly, this whole place was a hazard. It was amazing.

I picked up a bowl of worms with a shiver, moving it away from the edge of the counter. "You really need to do some organizing in here, I don't understand how you can find anything you need in this chaos." I called out. My toe jammed into a stack of cloths that was piled in the middle of the floor.

Kizzi sighed dramatically from behind the workbench. "It only looks like chaos to you because your brain didn't create it. This all makes perfect sense to me! Watch this. Quiz me. I'll close my eyes and find exactly what I'm looking for. What'll it be?"

"Uh, okay, weirdo... How about dried dragonfly wings?" I asked skeptically.

Kizzi pinched her eyes shut and stuck her arms out. "Wings... wings... last time I used a wing was yesterday when I made that anti-nausea potion for Old Man Wilbur, they were in the barrel under the..."

Kizzi tripped over a carton, and I caught her before she could faceplant into a cauldron full of boiling green liquid. I was her prince, here to rescue her and save the day!

"You dumb ass! See, I told you. By the way, you should've just done that with your eyes open, it would have proven your point just fine," I said, pulling her upright.

"Yeah, whatever, those damn sprites won't cut me a break. I swear they keep moving everything! See, I could've sworn that I left this basket of tree bark back behind my desk but now it's on the table with the cryptids. I would never do that! I keep flammable materials away from bug parts on purpose. I'm constantly putting things back where they belong, it's exhausting!"

"You've been pretty busy lately, right? With all the madness that's going on in Moonvale?"

"Yes!!" Kizzi exclaimed, flailing her arms dramatically. "I swear everyone has needed my help! It's a pain in the ass!" She glanced at me when I let out a quiet huff. "Not you, babycakes, you know I love helping you." She patted me on the cheek and left behind a smear of something warm and viscous. I wiped it off as quickly as possible.

"You know I can help you, right? I'm an expert at organizing random bits and bobs. You've seen my shop, it's flawless! Er, I mean–it used to be flawless!" Kizzi snorted out loud, so I amended. "Okay fine, maybe I know what you mean by that organized chaos thing. But at least when I misplace things it doesn't matter to anyone but myself. You could really do some damage. No offense," I said, gesturing to my colored hair.

"You look fabulous, and you know it. But you're right, I need to get this shit under control."

"You do. At least we've got each other's backs."

"Forever and always, bestie. Now, you know I love you, but I need you to get out of my hair so I can trip over barrels and make messes in peace. If you see any sprites on your way out, give them a one-two-punch for me."

"Yeah, yeah, sure Kiz. I'll beat up some tiny harmless creatures for you." I rolled my eyes. "To the moons!"

Her voice called after me. "To the suns!"

CHAPTER 18

Fiella

After what felt like endless hours of work, the main structure of my shop had finally been repaired, and it was wonderful to feel like the walls weren't caving in on me anymore. The claustrophobic feeling wasn't as suffocating.

I had my arms full of devastatingly broken trinkets when my door opened with a chime of the bell. I had just installed it the day before, and it was unexpectedly comforting to hear the bright, tinkling sound again. My heart sped in my chest.

"Welcome to Fiella's Finds! I'm Fiella! I don't really have anything for sale right now but if you let me know what you need, I can try to find it and have it ready for you in a few weeks!" I called out to the customer. The pile in my arms was too tall to see past.

"Uh, thank you. Do you have any extremely large stone bowls?"

I knew that smooth, deep voice.

Redd. Of course. I hadn't had any new customers since

the incident and I was beginning to actually hallucinate them. Of course nobody would want to shop here right now. Nobody *could* shop here right now. The place was a shit show.

Though I was disappointed, I was also strangely relieved. Redd's presence had become somewhat of a comfort. A new routine. Something to distract me, soothing some of the sharp edges of my aching chest. My skin prickled in awareness.

"Oh. Redd. It's you."

"It's me. Don't sound so excited about it, you'll give me a big head. Need more hands?" he asked. His voice was much closer now.

"Your head is already big enough as it is." I stepped out of his reach. "I've got it, I've got it, go grab the next stack. We're taking the trash out today!"

He chuckled quietly. "Yes, ma'am." I turned in time to catch a glimpse of him as he saluted me sarcastically. Smart ass.

"Oh, shut up," I tossed back at him. "Put those muscles to good use and grab some of the heavy stuff. Let's go."

We spent the next few hours hauling all the unsalvageable bits to the wheelbarrow I'd stationed out front.

It was almost pleasant, the way we worked together. Redd didn't always talk much, but he sure did listen. And I could tell that he truly listened because every once in a while, he would toss my own words back to me.

I was surprised when he remembered the story I had told him about how my Ma had loved collecting animal figurines from different towns, and how he had recognized the broken bits of a clay horse that she would have loved.

By the end of the day, the shop had a lot more floor space available, and all the rotten lumber had been disposed of. Everything broken had been hauled away. The torn tapestries, the crushed pottery, the mangled historical books–it was all gone.

My back and shoulders were burning like the heat of the dual suns, and I was exhausted.

I was trying not to mentally calculate the value of all I had lost. It was devastating. Thousands of silvers worth of hand-selected items destroyed in one fell swoop. The items I had managed to save were not enough to cheer me up.

Whoever had cursed me like this deserved a massive kick in the ass. I'd be sure to deliver it personally as soon as I figured out who the culprit was.

The beetles hadn't seemed to infiltrate any of the other businesses in town–I was the only victim. At least my neighbors had been spared the agony of mass destruction. Goblet-half-full.

It wasn't even just the money that caused my soul to ache. It was the memories that had been lost. The priceless finds. The one-of-a-kind treasures that could never be replaced. I had traveled far and wide to obtain my inventory, placed orders with the most esteemed of traveling merchants, and every piece was special.

This wound would take a long time to heal.

I said my farewells to Redd before my anger and sadness could boil over or I could take it out on him. I'd already blown up on the vampire a few times more than was polite, if I kept exploding on him, he would stop coming around, and the thought of that left a strangely sour taste in my mouth.

I needed the help.

I wanted the company.

Maybe I needed the company too.

I shoved my hand into the next mailbox I passed, a habit I had picked up over the last few weeks. Relief flooded my veins when my hand found crisp, cool paper. My constant checking had finally paid off.

Dear One,

I have not heard from you in a while. Too long.

Please write to me when you can.

Yours,
Two

Guilt tugged at me. I had completely forgotten that it was my turn to write. I had left the previous letter tucked under my watering jug and neglected to pen a response.

The fact that my penpal wrote me another letter anyway brought butterflies to my stomach.

CHAPTER 19
Fiella

I dreamt of magical mailboxes, fingers stained with ink, and kind, mysterious strangers.

After waking later than I normally would, I bundled up and headed to the shop. I noticed that the air somehow felt even colder than it had yesterday. We were supposed to be headed toward the mild season, not back to the freeze season. Ugh!

If the mild season didn't hit soon, Moonvale would miss the wave of tourists, and that would be disastrous for us all.

The wind was so frigid it was painful on my face, and the air felt like shards of glass as I breathed it into my nose. I had to blink rapidly so my eyeballs wouldn't frost over.

I made it to shop as fast as my legs would carry me without actually breaking into a run. It wasn't snowing, but the air certainly smelled like ice and darkness.

Redd was already waiting by the front door when I arrived, bouncing on his toes and holding himself stiffly.

"Gods, Fiella! Took you long enough, it's *freezing!*" he

snapped at me through chattering teeth. I tried to ignore how nice my name sounded in his mouth, even with the chattering. His lips were blue, and he had his arms wrapped tightly around himself. Someone needed to get this man a warmer cloak.

"Don't worry honey, Fiella's here to save the day," I grumbled back as I tried to still my shaking fingers long enough to fit the key into the lock.

I tucked my satchel in closer to my side. I didn't mention the fact that I had stopped at the bakery for pastries on my way. I figured that the news wouldn't go over well under the current circumstances. Even this shocking cold wasn't enough to disrupt my morning ritual.

Redd crowded so close behind me that I could feel his breath on the side of my face. Impatient vampire. I caught a hint of his mint and sandalwood scent and had to stop myself from inhaling more noticeably.

We both rushed inside as soon as the door was opened, slamming it shut behind us to keep the devilishly cold air out.

As we stood there, blowing hot breath onto our fingers and trying to regain blood flow in our extremities, I caught the sight of a snowflake lazily drifting to the ground from the corner of my eye. Weird–it didn't snow often in Moonvale, and never this late into the season.

Whatever, I was sure it would pass. It was probably only a few wayward flakes.

Sookie trotted over and rubbed her head against my ankles, meowing loudly. She even briefly rubbed up against Redd. Traitor. She was never affectionate to others like she was to me, it was our own sacred bond.

She had been in a strange mood ever since the beetle incident. I guess I couldn't blame her.

"Well, let's defrost a little and then get to work. If we finish repairing the loft today, we might be able to finally get started on those new shelves," I mentioned hopefully. Redd had convinced me to lay wood over my previously stone floors, and that had slowed our repair progress. As had the stone reinforcements on all four walls.

This was taking much longer than I had expected, but I wasn't necessarily upset about it. I subtly glanced at Redd.

He grumbled an agreement, eventually removing his cloak with reluctance. He was clearly not built for the cold. "You should get one of those enchanted fireplaces in here. It's fucking *cold*."

"Do I look like I'm made of silvers? Those things are expensive," I muttered back. "Toughen up. It's not that cold."

"Says the local. You forget I'm not from here. I've never been this cold in my *life*."

I held my arms out sarcastically. "Awww, you poor thing. Need me to warm you up?"

He shot me a glare. "No. I'll live."

I let my arms fall back to my sides with a snort. "I sure hope so. It would be so embarrassing to have to tell everyone such a strong and fearsome vampire dropped dead from a little chill."

"Oh great, she's got jokes," he grumbled.

"Get to work, frosty. We've got lots to accomplish today."

His exasperated sigh was extremely satisfying.

Redd and I lost ourselves in our newfound routine, not noticing the hours as they passed. I didn't want to open the door to take the garbage outside, so we made a pile by the door to deal with later.

I was growing to appreciate the grumpy vampire's company more and more, as much as I had tried to avoid it. He would be leaving eventually, he made it clear that he wasn't here to stay, and it would be a waste of time to grow attached.

He was just taking a break from Sunhaven, before he either went back or moved on to somewhere new.

I couldn't figure him out. He spoke fondly of his home, but he didn't seem to want to go back any time soon. He didn't sound passionate about traveling, either, like my Ma and Pa were. He just reluctantly accepted the fact that he was moving from place to place.

It was strange.

"You don't talk about your home much, aren't you from Sunhaven? I travel there often; you guys have some lovely shops. Do you miss it?" I asked while scooping up a pile of dust. The dust was never ending. I needed to invest in an anti-dust crystal for the shop, whenever the silvers were flowing again.

He took a moment to think before answering, his hands busy sorting a pile of wooden boards.

"I do miss it sometimes. There's not much to tell, though. Nobody wanted me around there anymore. It was for the best that I left." I couldn't see his face, but he sounded a little too nonchalant. Like he was forcing it.

I scoffed. "I'm sure that's not true. I bet there are tons of people missing you right now. What about your family? Or your friends? Or any lady friends?" That last part slipped out before I could hold it back. Whoops.

He glanced at me from the corner of his eye, a frown pulling at his mouth.

"Trust me, they're happy that I'm not around to screw things up for them anymore." He turned his back on me, moving over to begin hammering down the new loft stairs.

I couldn't help but notice that he didn't deny having lady friends back home. *I'll have to pry more information out of him about that later.*

I stepped into his eyeline and tapped him on the arm, forcing him to look at me.

"No way. Please explain. It's not like you're a creepy murderer or anything, you're just a little bit of an asshole. No offense. There's no way they were happy to see you go," I insisted. The thought of Redd having nobody missing him back home made my heart ache in a strange way.

Everyone deserved to have people who cared about them enough to miss them fiercely.

He took a deep breath, hesitated for just a moment, and then he began to speak.

I removed my hand from his arm and stepped back, and my hand felt cold. I shivered as a chill traveled up my arm and down my spine.

"It's hard to explain," he started. "First it was the small things. Minor shop mishaps. Tools going missing. Things of that nature."

"Sure, that sounds pretty normal," I responded, confused.

He shook his head, frustrated. "It didn't stay that way. Things got worse."

"How so?"

"Things just started to get bad. Really bad. Everywhere I went. I don't know how it happened, but somehow, I became this... this bad luck charm."

"Bad luck charm," I stated. "I don't understand."

He gritted his teeth and ran his hand through his hair, mussing the strands. "I don't understand it either, Fiella, but I know what I saw. The town was falling apart because of me. My friends were getting sick. My family's business was suffering. *Everyone* was suffering. So I left. I fled. I was hoping that if I left, then my family and my friends would be spared from whatever curse was following me."

I took another step back, feeling slightly woozy. "Okay..."

"That's how I ended up here. I crossed the Barren Lands because I was *sure* that the bad luck wouldn't be able to follow me. But somehow, some way, it did." His cheeks reddened, and I could hear his heart thumping from across the room. He stared at me anxiously.

I leaned forward, my hands on my knees. My vision began to darken at the edges, panic trying to claw under my skin.

He had somehow become the harbinger of bad luck, setting off an unfortunate chain of events wherever he went. He fled Sunhaven to spare his family and neighbors from further tragedy. He traveled to Moonvale to try to escape the misfortune.

He brought the bad luck here with him.

He believed he was the cause of my shop travesty. My massive financial loss. The destruction of my livelihood.

He believed it was all, somehow, his fault.

For probably the first time in my life, I was speechless.

"Oh...kay." I let out a massive breath, my cheeks puffing out.

"Okay. Okay. Hey, it could just be a huge coincidence," I said, though I wasn't sure if I believed that myself. I forced myself to straighten up and breathe.

One incident, or two, or three, could be explained as a coincidence. What he was describing sounded like much more than that.

He did arrive in town right before everything started happening...

I had crossed paths with him right before...

I tried to hold back the wave of anger and resentment that threatened to wash over me. I tried to stop the claws of panic from piercing their way into my mind, my chest. If what Redd was describing was true, then maybe the worst incident of my life really was his fault.

I didn't want to blame him, but I couldn't stop my thoughts from spiraling. I didn't know what to think.

He stared at me for a long time, a crease between his brows and his hands folded together in front of him. "You know what, maybe I'll just go. I'll come back tomorrow, and we'll wrap this up here," he eventually murmured.

"That's probably for the best," I choked out. "Thank you."

"I'm sorry, Fiella. I didn't mean for any of this to happen." His voice quaked slightly.

I didn't respond, my eyes glued to the floor. When he

turned to face the door, he froze in place, gaping at the window.

While we had been absorbed in conversation, we hadn't noticed the shop slowly getting darker. Had night fallen already?

No, that wasn't night. What we saw out the window was absolutely nothing. Blackness.

"Well, fuck," Redd proclaimed.

I couldn't have said it better myself.

"Looks like we're snowed in."

CHAPTER 20
Redd

F uck.

Fuck fuck fuck. This was *not* good.

I had been planning to make my escape, feeling raw and ragged after finally explaining the truth to Fiella, and now I was stuck.

Apparently, the unlucky streak hadn't broken yet.

My stomach, sensing that I was already at rock bottom, decided to knock me even lower. It let out a loud growl that was echoed by the feeling of molten nails dragging down my throat. The sensation was almost enough to knock me onto my knees. My vision tunneled, darkening around the edges.

I *had* to get out of here.

I yanked the door open, hoping to the fates that my escape would still be possible, but all I did was let in a massive pile of snow that refilled instantly. I couldn't even see where it had come from.

My heart sinking past the floor, I realized that there was no way I was getting out any time soon.

Grumbling, I scooped out as much snow as I could, kicking at what I could reach, and slammed the door shut. The soon-to-be puddle on the floor was the least of our concerns at the moment.

I turned slowly to find Fiella watching me, wringing her hands in front of her. Her shimmery nails glinted in the lantern light. She looked anxious, in a way that made me want to comfort her. It was unsettling. I hated it.

"Well," She stated awkwardly. "Maybe it'll clear soon?"

"We both know that's not happening tonight," I snapped, unable to control my temper. My throat was disintegrating, my nerves fraying one by one. It was agony.

"Okay, okay, well... I've got some extra pastries that we can share, so at least we won't starve." She held her hands up placatingly.

Pastries. Pastries! While pastries would help the growling of my stomach, they wouldn't touch the growing inferno in my throat that was slowly taking over my every thought.

I still hadn't gotten my hands on any thirst tonic, and I had planned on ordering a blood ale (or four) at the diner with my evening meal to take the edge off. *Well, I'm screwed.*

I gritted my teeth, my fangs abrading the inside of my mouth. I could ignore the mind-numbing agony in my throat for one more night.

I had to.

Fiella grabbed her sack of pastries from under the counter, along with a canteen of water, and guided us to the newly repaired sitting nook. She hesitantly handed me a croissant.

I tried to ignore the tense, awkward atmosphere, but after dropping the truth bomb I had earlier, that felt almost impossible.

We just had to make it through the night, and then we could go our separate ways.

I shoved the pastry into my mouth so hastily I hardly tasted it. It could've been boysenberry, or dirt, for all I noticed. It sat like lead in my stomach, offering no satisfaction except for the fact that it took up space. At least the chasm was no longer empty.

Fiella handed me a cookie that I inhaled just as quickly.

"So..." She said to break the silence. "What should we do now? Should we get some more work done? Continue discussing how you could've possibly been the cause of the disaster we have been working to repair for weeks?" Her voice was sharp, but not unkind.

We had already worked ourselves ragged today, and I could tell by the way she was subtly flexing her fingers and rubbing her lower back when she thought I wasn't watching that her body was exhausted. Not to mention the hollows settling in under her eyes.

I couldn't even determine how I was feeling, the incessant thirst overwhelming all my senses. I was in Hell's Realm.

I clenched my jaw, shoving my fists into my eyes and massaging, trying to relieve the pressure radiating from my fangs throughout my skull. "Anything. Something distracting, please," I gritted out.

"Well," she tapped her chin in thought. "When I need a distraction, I always pick up a book. Diving into another world, another story, is the best way to keep your mind off your own."

I dropped my hands to my side, glancing at her face. Though her expression was still tense, she was staring at me hopefully.

"That's... that's a great idea, actually. I love reading."

Her eyebrows shot to her hairline. "You do?"

I scoffed. "Don't look so surprised. I'm offended."

She waved her hand. "No, no, I just didn't expect it. You're such a big, burly, gruff vampire, I can't imagine you curled up on a comfy cushion with a book in your hand and a cup of tea beside you."

"What do you think I do in my spare time? Smash rocks?"

"Honestly, yes. Something like that."

I shot her a glare, surprised to find that she was gently smiling, a teasing glint in her eyes. "Very funny. I have quite the collection of books back home in Sunhaven."

Fiella leaned her hip against the counter, crossing her arms in front of her. "What kind of books do you like to read, mister sophisticated literature man?"

I rolled my eyes. "Mysteries, mostly. Anything with adventure and suspense. I like to see how mysteries unfold, and how they're solved."

She nodded thoughtfully. "Yeah, that seems like you."

"And how about you? Where do your book tastes fall?"

She barked out a laugh, her cheeks reddening slightly. "Romance, mostly. Anything with a love story."

I nodded sagely. "The raunchy stuff or the family-friendly stuff?"

She laughed again, the sound more endearing this time.

"Raunchy, of course. Though I'll pick up anything if it's got love in it. I'm a hopeless romantic."

"I think I remember seeing a box of newer books that had survived the collapse, where did we put those? Think there are any romantic mysteries in there?"

"Of course, who do you think I am? I keep only the best in my inventory." She fumbled around for a bit before triumphantly lifting a box from the ground.

The books in the box had survived the collapse relatively unscathed, only earning a few bends and scratches. We situated ourselves on the chairs in the sitting area, prepared to read the evening away and pass the time. I ended up with *Murder on the Mountain Pass*, while Fiella selected *The Siren and the Sorcerer*, which depicted a kissing couple on the cover.

The tale was surprisingly riveting, and it ensnared my attention quickly. I would have to purchase this one.

Sometime later, when I noticed Fiella nodding off while sitting upright, I decided we could at least try to get some sleep. She was too stubborn to make that call herself.

Or at least *she* could get some sleep. There was no way I was going to be able to get any significant rest while my throat was shredding itself apart.

We pulled the cushions from the comfy chairs, laid them flat, and gathered a few throw blankets to cover up with.

It was lucky that this shop seemed to have every item under the suns, even after most of it had been destroyed.

Fiella extinguished the lantern and darkness descended upon us. The silence was tense and awkward—every rustle of fabric a disturbance and every breath deafening.

"Goodnight, Fiella," I murmured, just a few feet away from her in the darkness.

"Goodnight, stranger," She mumbled back sleepily.

I couldn't help the pained smile that tugged at my mouth. Luckily, she wouldn't be able to see it with her eyes closed.

As her breaths evened out and she eventually drifted off to sleep, I braced myself for hours of misery. My thoughts were beginning to slow, feeling strangely heavy. And my fangs *hurt*.

I caught myself wondering where in the realms that cat had wandered off to–I could have sworn she was here a few hours ago.

This gods damned snow better clear out soon.

CHAPTER 21
Fiella

I awoke sometime later to a strange clacking sound, as fast as a hummingbird's wings and piercing in the calm of the shop.

What in the realms...

I slowly sat up, determined to figure out what that sound could possibly be.

It didn't take me long to find the source. Redd was laying on his cushions a few feet away, curled in on himself, and his teeth were chattering like he was freezing to death. A steady stream of blood was dripping from the corner of his mouth and onto the floor from where his own fangs had punctured the flesh of his lip.

I sleepily rubbed my hands over my arms and didn't feel any goosebumps. It wasn't *that* cold. Unless...

I crawled over to him to investigate. He hardly even seemed to notice my approach. He was clutching his throat and his whole body was wracked with tremors.

I froze. I had seen these symptoms before and had felt

them myself when I tried to stretch my time between thirst tonics.

This was bloodlust–the raw, animalistic, murderous state that a vampire could slip into if thirst wasn't properly taken care of.

I took a deep breath to shed my apprehension.

I grabbed his shoulder, gently shaking him to get his attention and to wake him from his trance.

"Redd, hey, snap out of it. You're hurting yourself; you've got to relax." I shook him a little harder. "You're okay. You're just a little thirsty."

Redd surprised me by leaping at me, faster than I'd ever seen him move. Faster than I'd seen *any* creature move.

He slammed into me like a battering ram, launching me onto my back and trapping me with his knees pinning my hips and his hands latched onto my neck. My breath *whooshed* out of me at the impact. Luckily, I had my own cushions to land on, or my brains would've been scrambled.

I bucked and flailed, trying to get the feral vampire off me. It was no use. I was strong, but I was no match for him at that moment.

He was a hunter, and I was his prey.

His eyes were hazy, unfocused, his sclera black as the night sky. A wild creature with nothing but blood on his mind. His primal instincts taking over. The monster creeping in.

He bared his teeth, letting out a primal snarl that made me shiver, my heart speeding into a gallop. His fangs elongated in threat, promising to drain whoever they sank into.

He leaned forward, his eyes never quite making contact with mine. Slowly, so slowly. His weight pressed me in the ground. My lungs struggled to pull in air. I fought against the instinct to fight him, to inflict damage, to flee no matter what it took.

He was lost in the bloodlust, but I still didn't want to hurt him.

My vision darkened at the edges. My galloping heart was the only sound in the silent room, a deafening bass drum.

As his face brushed the side of the neck, he inhaled deeply and seemed to shake some sense into himself. His body tensed on top of me, his muscles freezing. I counted down the seconds. My lungs screamed for air and my thoughts began to swim.

Ten.

Fifteen.

Twenty.

His hands finally loosened their punishing grip on my neck. I greedily sucked in air as his fingers relaxed one by one, his thumbs brushing over the column of my throat in a strange, gentle caress. He exhaled in a harsh huff, blowing my loose hair back off of my face.

He was shaking from restraint, practically vibrating with the effort it took him to keep his fangs out of my jugular.

"Fiella..." His voice was a strangled, half apology and half plea.

His eyes met mine, his pupils blown so wide they blended into the darkness overtaking his eyes. Not a hint of brown to be seen.

How long had it been since he had taken any thirst tonic? Hells, he had to be absolutely suffering. Has he been in pain this whole time? No wonder he was so... grumpy.

Vampires didn't drink from other vampires unless they were closely bonded, and my instincts rebelled at the idea, but this seemed like the right time to make an exception.

It was a necessity. Nothing more, nothing less. Redd just needed some blood, and then he would be back to his normal self.

I couldn't stop the feeling of warmth from spreading through me from head to toe. I had drunk from partners in the past, sure, but I had always regretted it. Relationships were never the same afterwards. I had never allowed anyone to drink from me, though.

I knew what was probably going to happen. I knew that the second his fangs pierced my flesh, I would probably crave more. I knew that something wild and foreign would ignite in my blood, would burn through my flesh, and would convince my own fangs that they needed a taste as well.

The thing was, I didn't care. I didn't care what would happen, I didn't care that this was something frowned upon, I didn't care what any of the aftermath would be. I just wanted to ease Redd's suffering, to give him some relief.

And maybe, I also wanted to satisfy my own selfish curiosity.

He would do the same for me, if the situation was reversed.

Silly, stubborn vampire. Should've drank the blue-hair thirst tonic when I offered to share.

I took a deep breath, pulling the air all the way to the very base of my lungs.

"It's okay, Redd, just do it. Bite me."

145

CHAPTER 22

Redd

The world was red. And death. And pain.

There was nothing but blood. Red blood, black blood, green blood. I saw flashes of it, dripping and thick and sliding down the back of my throat and filling me like a well. Filling me entirely. Infiltrating my every cell, my every thought, my entire being.

Pain.

Pain.

Blood. Need blood.

No. Not this blood. Not her.

Not the blood that smells like warmth and berries.

I snarled at the swirling thoughts in my mind.

"It's okay, Redd, just do it. Bite me."

The words pierced the haze I was trapped in. Fiella. This was Fiella. The feisty vampire that owned the trinket shop.

The woman I couldn't seem to scrape my thoughts away from.

NO. That was the bloodlust talking.

My muscles were steel and concrete– it took the power of a thousand suns for me to slowly peel my hands from her delicate throat.

Must get off. Must crawl away. Must escape.

My vision was tunneled, but I knew I had to get away from the woman on the floor. I spit a mouthful of saliva off to the side, trying to force my fangs into retreating into my gums.

Long, delicate fingers wrapped around my wrist. My gaze snapped to a set of amber-colored eyes.

She slowly pulled my hands back toward her neck. Gently.

"It's okay, Redd. I know how it goes. I'm a vampire too, remember? Just drink from me a little, it'll make you feel so much better."

Her pupils were blown wide, and she was slightly panting. I couldn't tell if it was fear or something else that was causing her body to react strangely, but I could hardly focus on that with the red haze tugging at my senses.

All I could think about was her blood, hot and sweet and pumping rapidly through her veins. Drumming, thundering, deafening.

It took me a moment to register what she was saying.

"No!" I snarled. I couldn't. I shouldn't.

Mine. Mine. Mine.

Woah, where did that come from? Fiella was *not* mine.

I shook my head to clear my thoughts and tried to pull myself off of her again.

Her grip tightened, and her nails dug into my flesh. Her face tightened into a mask of determination.

My fierce creature. *No! Not mine. What the fuck, Redd, snap out of it.*

"Just do it, you stubborn man. We're both adults here, and the fates know how long we're going to be stuck here together. Just get it over with while you still have some rationality left in you, so you don't end up ripping my throat open later and bleeding me dry." Her voice was strangely breathy.

She shivered at that last statement, a flash of alarm crossing her features.

No. I would never rip her throat open. That was absurd.

My thoughts were at war.

The darkness was creeping in again, muddling my thoughts further.

After long seconds, I decided that she was right, and I couldn't hold myself back anymore.

I leaned forward, taking a deep inhale of her sweet berry scent, braced myself, and let my fangs sink into the silky skin of her throat.

Oh, fuck.

CHAPTER 23

Fiella

Ouch.

I had never been bit by another vampire before, but gods damn did it sting.

Wait.

Oh.

Oh.

My veins flooded with warmth, and the sensation pooled in my stomach.

Redd latched on harder, letting out a sound somewhere between a growl and a groan. I could hear his heart thundering as he swallowed me down, pulling my blood into his mouth, his throat working rhythmically.

He adjusted his position on top of me, trying to get a better angle to access my vein while he drank.

He threaded his fingers into my hair, lifting my head and tilting it slightly.

One of his knees slid between my legs. I jolted at the contact, heat roiling in my core.

Redd's weight settled on top of me as his fangs sunk

deeper into my skin, pain blending seamlessly with pleasure. He pinned me down, restricting my movements and holding me hostage.

He was the hunter, and I was his prey.

I writhed beneath him, trapping the moan that threatened to escape my throat. I didn't want him to know how much I was enjoying this, but my body betrayed me.

I ground my hips against his leg as the blinding pleasure of his bite flowed through me, mindless with bliss. He growled and yanked my head back even further, and the bite of pain in my scalp heightened the delicious sensations.

Long seconds passed, and I hoped he would never stop.

I prayed to the Old Gods that he would never stop.

But eventually he did.

I felt his fangs slip from my throat, and his tongue swiped over the mark, soothing the sting.

My head was spinning, my mind blurry and my thoughts jumbled.

My vision faded into darkness as I slipped into a deep, dark sleep.

CHAPTER 24

Fiella

When I woke again, I could only tell it was morning by the thin streams of light creeping in through the window over the mountains of snow. My eyes felt gritty, not wanting to open. I rubbed the drowsiness out of my them as I slowly sat up.

My head swam dizzyingly before I steadied myself again.

Redd was sitting in the chair, his ankle propped up on his knee, reading the same book he had started last night. Something about murders. He glanced at me, casually, as though nothing had happened last night. Even his hair was tucked back into its usual tidy shape.

Was that a dream?

I hesitantly reached for my throat, and sure enough, there was a sore spot right above my jugular. His eyes tracked my hand, and his jaw clenched. His cheeks reddened slightly.

He cleared his throat. "Good morning," he gritted out,

dragging his eyes away from my throat and back to the book in his lap.

Oh, so we were playing it casually, huh? Great. Two could play that game.

"Good morning," I mumbled, smoothing down my snarled hair and pulling myself up off the ground. "Sleep alright?" I glanced at him as I gathered the cushions and placed them back onto the chair.

"Oh, yeah, like a baby," he said.

I just hummed in response. *Infuriating creature.*

I freshened myself up in the washroom, split another pastry between Redd and I, and busied myself with organizing a box of tiny seashells.

"So... are you okay?" I asked awkwardly, unsure how to broach the topic.

Redd cleared his throat and kept his eyes on the book in his lap, though I did notice the flush spreading to his ears. "Yes. I'm fine. Thank you, by the way." His eyes flitted up to meet mine for just a moment before they danced away again in embarrassment.

"You're welcome. You would've done the same for me if the situations were reversed. We don't have to make it weird or anything."

"Right, right. It's not weird."

"Not weird at all."

"Nope."

I forced a tense smile to my face and returned my attention to the idle task at hand. After working in awkward silence for what felt like hours, I heard something that sounded like a voice.

"Woah! Did you hear that?" I asked Redd, leaping to my feet.

"Hear what?"

"That!" I was positive that I heard it that time.

"Fiella! Fi are you in there! I went by your cottage, but you weren't there! Oh, gods, you better not be dead!"

Kizzi! I had never been so relieved to hear the witch's voice. My heart leapt into my throat. We were saved!

"I'm here, Kiz! Not dead, just a little stuck!"

"How does it look out there?" Redd yelled behind me.

Kizzi let out a squawk. "Redd! You're in there too? Oh, how interesting!"

My cheeks flushed scarlet. I avoided looking in Redd's direction like my life depended on it. I would not give him the satisfaction of seeing me flustered when he was playing it so cool.

"Yeah, yeah, whatever, just answer the question! How does it look out there? If you were able to approach the shop, I'm guessing it's starting to melt?" I asked.

"Oh, right! I've been working with the other witches to melt paths through town, this whole situation reeks of dark sorcery. We'll get you out of there in a jiff!"

I couldn't hear her footsteps fading away, but I was pretty sure she had left.

Thank the gods, we were getting out of here.

I turned to see that Redd was already looking at me. He quickly looked away, clearing his throat.

"Well, that's that," he murmured. "Thank you, again. I mean it. My thirst has never gotten that bad before." He finally met my eyes.

"I'm glad you're feeling better." I winked to lighten the tension in the air.

The corner of his mouth lifted slightly. "Oh yes, *much* better." He licked his lips, his eyes flicking back to my neck. "You're delicious, by the way."

That startled me. I mean, of course I was, but I was not expecting him to come out and say it like that. My jaw dropped.

His mouth lifted into a full-blown smile, flashing his sharp fangs that had been embedded in my flesh just last night. He was unfairly handsome. It was distracting.

This time I was the one clearing my throat. "Thank you? I'd say it's my own personal recipe, but I don't think that would make any sense." I was trying to rein in my reaction as much as possible. I consciously tried to slow my heartbeat, breathing in slowly through my nose and out through my mouth. I didn't want to give him the satisfaction of hearing my heart rate pick up.

He let out a low laugh. "I couldn't help myself; it was low hanging fruit."

Was he picking on me? I was definitely rubbing off on him. *Figuratively and literally.* I snorted at my personal silent joke.

Our conversation was interrupted by a loud meow from the unfinished loft.

"Sookie? Sookie! Where in Hell's Realm have you been?" I asked the cat as I scooped her up and snuggled her into my chest. "I thought you must have made it out before the snow shut us in, I haven't seen you in ages!"

She glanced at the back door, purring softly. Ah. Smart cat.

Sure enough, the tenacious creature had dug her way through the snow and entered through the back door, a trail of wet paw prints betraying the path she had taken.

"Well, I guess if the cat can do it, we can too," Redd stated. He wasn't wrong.

I shrugged. It was the best plan we had come up with so far, and I was itching to get out of here.

We grabbed a few stone bowls, bundled up into our cloaks, and got to work, digging our way free.

I didn't recognize the strange pang in my chest I felt at the thought of getting out of here. Surely that wasn't disappointment.

CHAPTER 25
Redd

After what felt like hours of scooping snow, sweat dripping down our backs, we finally made a path large enough that we could crawl through it and escape the shop.

My breaths were heaving from the effort. The air going down my throat felt smooth and comfortable–a massive relief from the sawing sensation that had been plaguing me the last few weeks.

I was too relieved to be annoyed that my clothes were soaked with melted snow.

As I turned to leave, Fiella headed back to the counter.

"Forget something?" I asked her. Her satchel was hanging by her hip, so it wasn't that.

"I just need to finish something really quick; you go on ahead," she called out distractedly.

Huh. Must've been an important invoice or something, if it was enough to keep her in the shop for even longer. I shrugged. I didn't waste time trying to understand the beguiling woman.

I pulled my cloak tighter around myself, braced for the chill, and crawled out into the fresh air. The dual suns were shockingly bright when reflecting off the white mountains of snow. I took a few deep breaths before I could take in my surroundings.

My jaw dropped and my eyebrows raised as I turned in a circle, taking in the massive glittering piles. The stuff looked fluffy and soft, but I knew from my experience digging out of Fiella's Finds that it was quite dense.

It never snowed back home in Sunhaven. I knew what snow was from the stories I had heard and books I had read, but I had never experienced it firsthand. I decided that snow was the absolute *worst*.

I passed Kizzi and the other witches, whose names I couldn't remember, as I headed away from town square. The short, green witch waggled her eyebrows at me.

"So, Mister Redd," Kizzi asked innocently. "Enjoy your sleepover?"

I waved her off. "Oh, shut up," I grumbled.

"I bet you didn't sleep much, huh?" she pushed.

"It wasn't like that, gods. Don't go spreading that rumor." I glanced at the other witches, who were looking around and pretending like they weren't eavesdropping. "Thanks for the help, by the way," I said pointedly, looking at the tunnel Fiella and I had dug ourselves.

She turned around dismissively, responding over her shoulder. "Oh, quit whining, I knew you two would figure it out. Or I'd come save you eventually."

I hurried away before I could hear any more, itching to escape.

The town was sparkling, every inch of it either coated

with ice crystals or piled with powdery snow. It would have been decent to look at if it wasn't so gods damned *cold*.

Something about this monumental change in weather seemed unnatural. Like perhaps it was... magical. From what I had heard from the townsfolk, Moonvale was supposed to be pleasant and temperate this time of year. This was as far from pleasant as I could possibly imagine.

I thought about tracking down Mayor Tommins for another work assignment, but I figured he had bigger things to worry about today. I could use the break, anyways. My body was exhausted, and the relief of finally satisfying my thirst had my muscles feeling lax and lazy.

Glancing around, I wasn't sure how Tommins was going to manage this mess. The town was surely used to the cold and the snow, but this amount of coverage would bury even the hardiest of towns.

Moonvale was clearly not equipped for snowfall like this.

The snow was to my knees, and I was tall, so I couldn't imagine any smaller folk making it anywhere today without staying on one of the melted paths. I stomped toward my destination, raising my feet high between each step, feeling like a fool.

I made my way towards the diner, but a path hadn't been cleared yet and I couldn't see any evidence of footfalls, so I assumed it was closed. As a last-ditch effort, I plowed my way over to the grocery store.

I wasn't the best chef in the world, but I was able to keep myself fed if I needed to. I just preferred when other folk cooked instead. Sadly, though, my icebox was empty.

Luckily, the grocery store looked open. It was set on a

bit of a hill, and I could see light coming through the windows. Maybe I had finally exhausted the well of bad luck that seemed determined to drown me.

I knocked on the wood of the front door before pulling it open, just in case.

I waved at the friendly mothman who ran the store and set about finding ingredients for a decent meal. Now that the fire in my throat had eased, I could focus more on my stomach. Fiella's stash of pastries had been a minor relief, but the tarts only took the edge off my hunger–they hadn't come close to satisfying it.

"Hey there! I wasn't expecting to get any customers today, how in the realms did you make it here?" the mothman asked in a chipper voice.

"Desperate times call for desperate measures, or so they say," I responded with a forced smile. It wasn't the mothman's fault that this morning was so strange. We were *all* having a rough morning. "I just dragged myself through the snow. You flew here, I assume?"

"Yes." He shivered. "And I almost froze my wings off in the process. But duty calls." He waved his hand at the grocery shop.

"Well, I'm certainly grateful you did. Thanks man."

He simply nodded in response.

It was nice to be around other folk again without the urge to rip out any throats. I hardly even noticed his pulse fluttering under his thin skin.

I meandered through the aisles, pleasantly surprised by the variety in the stock. This store had *everything*. The inventory catered to a wide range of folk–I could see items for humans, for elves, for orcs, for sprites. They even sold bottled animal blood for vampires.

Thanks to Fiella, I wasn't very thirsty. I smiled wryly to myself. The thought made my body warm. Last night almost felt like a dream, I was so hazy with thirst. Some of the details were crystal clear, though. Like her sweet smell of warmth and berries, and the taste of her on my tongue.

Like the way I tossed her across the room like a sack of flour and pinned her down with my body.

I would have to apologize for that later, I had probably scared her. Hells, I had certainly scared myself. I had never lost control like that, at least not since I was a little.

I could have *killed* her.

I tucked my grocery haul close to my chest, braced myself to return to the frigid cold, and headed toward my cottage on the edge of town.

This was going to be a slow, cold walk.

When I finally made it to my destination, scraped my door open, and clambered inside, I was shocked to see a neatly folded piece of parchment sitting on my entryway table.

Ignoring the landslide of snow that would certainly cause a giant mess inside, I dropped my groceries onto the counter, snatched the letter, and began reading.

My friend Two,

You missed me, didn't you? I can't say I blame you. I would miss me too.

Don't worry, I didn't forget about you, I've just been busy and forgetful. I'm sorry.

If it helps, you haven't been far from my mind. I wonder about you often.

Anyways, I hope you have been staying happy and busy, and that you've been drinking as much of that disgusting golden ale as your heart desires.

Still here,
One

Whoever this person was, they made me smile harder than I had in a long time.

I grabbed my parchment, sat down, and started writing, the corners of my mouth lifted the entire time.

CHAPTER 26
Fiella

After Redd had fled the shop this morning, I'd penned my letter to my mysterious penpal and dropped it in the mailbox closest to my shop. The thing had been so piled with snow that I had to grab one of my stone bowls to scoop it free, but it was worth it.

My penpal brought some hope and much-needed happiness to my life, and I wouldn't let a little snow deprive me of that.

Kizzi, still working on clearing paths to the rest of the businesses in the area, looked at me like I was ridiculous, but surprisingly, she said nothing about my bizarre actions. I was sure I would be hearing about this later.

"To the moons, Kiz!" I called out to Kizzi, planning to make my escape back to my cottage so I could curl up on my couch and read romance novels for the rest of the evening. Gods knew I needed it.

"Woah, woah, woah, not so fast, bitch! Come help us! We could use some more hands!" Kizzi shouted after me.

"I don't have any magic, and you guys look like you've

got it handled! You're doing such a great job! I'm so proud of you!" I called back desperately, hoping a little flattery would work in my favor.

It did not. Kizzi just rolled her eyes at me and told me to pick up my damn stone bowl and start scooping paths the way I'd scooped out the mailbox. She also told me to quit being a lazy sack of shit.

She had a point.

Damn it. I should've just snuck out without saying anything. Now I was stuck. Again.

Against my will, I stayed to help.

By the time the dual suns had sunk past the horizon, my shoulders were on fire, my arms felt like liquid sacks, and I was *starving*.

The townsfolk had rallied to the occasion, and as we all worked together, we got the most destructive of the snow out of the way. We had managed to clear a path to every business surrounding the town square.

I demanded that Kizzi come with me to the diner so we could debrief. We had a *lot* to catch up on.

"Y ou've got to be fucking shitting me!" Kizzi gasped, a few ciders deep and laughing ridiculously.

"I'm not shitting anyone! He bit me! Right here, look!" I showed her the wounds on my throat for proof. They would be gone by tomorrow, but for now, the flesh on my neck was scabbed and mottled with bruising.

"Lemme see!" Kizzi grabbed my head and wrenched it to the side, almost snapping my neck in the process. The diner was crowded but we ignored any rude looks that other folk cast our way. They were just jealous that they weren't as cool and sexy and gorgeous as we were. And that they couldn't drink as many ciders as we could.

"See I told you! Sunk those fangs right in me! You should've seen him; he was all feral and wild and sexy. It was awesome," I babbled drunkenly.

"Sexy huh!" She winked at me, but it looked more like she was having an eyelid spasm. "So, was he good in bed?" She tried and failed to stifle giggles.

"Kiz! No!" I exclaimed, aghast. "I didn't mean to say sexy. I told you he's an asshole, he's just also pretty!" And strong. And helpful. And sometimes charming... But mostly an asshole. If only he was like my penpal, my penpal was so gods damned *nice*.

"You can sleep with him if he's an asshole, who cares!" She clutched my arm. "Just for funsies! It's been, what, a year since you stopped seeing that annoying wolf guy?"

I shook her grip off.

"Noooooooo I can't sleep with this one! He's leaving soon, and that is just a mess waiting to happen. I hate mess-es." I took another swig of cider. But he was pretty though. *I bet he would be a good kisser.* He was an excellent biter. Did that correlate? Probably.

I wish they had the lavender blueberry ciders today. This rosemary plum cider was great too, but nothing topped the lavender. I sipped the liquid again. Maybe rosemary was becoming my new favorite. It was growing on me.

We needed to order more fried potatoes. We were a little too tipsy. I couldn't seem to think in a straight line, and my word filter had long since loosened.

"So what if he leaves! That resolves the entire mess in one swoop. Like I said, just for funsiesssss. He's hot, and you're hot, who cares!" Kizzi fell off her stool and had to scramble back up, giggling the entire time.

A human man at the next table cleared his throat, glancing pointedly at us. Hater. He wished he was having as much fun as we were. I snarled at him, baring my fangs before turning back to Kizzi.

"What if I get attached? That would suck. Maybe I am already attached. I didn't mean that." I was speaking madness. I wasn't an attachment sort of person.

"Mind over matter, bestie!" Kizzi held her goblet out unsteadily.

Mind over matter. Mind over matter! "Cheers to that!" I cried.

We clanked our goblets, only spilling a little bit onto the table.

"How has your sorcery sleuthing been going! Catch any bad guys? Did you figure out who's out to get me? It might be Redd's fault..." My thoughts were jumbled all over the place.

"Woah. Lots of thoughts all at once. Okay." She placed her green hands on the table and looked me deep in the eyes. I recognized that face, that was her *I'm focusing* face.

"First of all, I'm way too drunk for so many details so I'll give you the gist now and the full story tomorrow."

"That's good enough for me. Continue." I assumed the same focused position.

"If you want to talk about messes, the sorcerers are the biggest mess of all!" She was practically shouting now. "They're just fucking things up all over the place!"

I slapped the table. "I know right! They're fucking up everything! How are they fucking up everything?"

"They've got to be behind it all! Everything. My sprites, your shop, the sicknesses, the mishaps, even the snow!" she explained.

I let that sink into my brain. "Woah.... Now that you mention it, that makes total sense. Do you think it's all tied together? Is all of it Redd's fault?"

Kizzi quirked her head. "I have no idea what that means but yes, we're prettyyyyy sure it's all linked somehow. Not sure how, but somehow!"

I slapped the table again. "Redd confessed last night that it was all him. That he got wrapped in some bad luck somehow, back at home I mean, his home, and he brought it with him. It followed him here like a puppy!"

Kizzi sighed, slumping in her stool. "Well, fuck. Maybe it is his fault. But that doesn't really make sense!" She rubbed her temples. "My brain is too slow right now; I can't think this through. Less thinking, more drinking."

"I can get behind that!"

CHAPTER 27
Fiella

I woke up, very late, with a letter sitting beside my head on my pillow. My thoughts were too muddled to care about how it had gotten there, I only felt the joy of hearing from my mysterious friend again.

Dear One,

I was going to say I was worried about you, that maybe you fell into a river and drowned, but sure. I guess I missed you.

I hope you have missed me too.

I have had a few ales lately, but after today, I need a boatload. Ten ales. All of the ales.

Things are getting even more complicated for me in this town. I hope the days have been smoother for you, my friend.

Read any good books lately? I started one recently that really intrigued me, it's about a murderous faerie that lives in the mountains.

Your friend,
Two

I smiled groggily and wobbled toward the table to pen a quick response.

When I finally made my way to the shop after scraping myself out of my cottage and tromping through the snow, my head was pounding. It felt like my brain had turned into an army of sprites that were trying to burst free.

Those ciders always got me. I might've had a *few* too many yesterday.

The shop was empty, aside from Sookie and me. I usually preferred it that way, but something about it felt strange today. Wrong. Like something was missing.

This snow needed to melt, and it needed to melt *fast*. If travel didn't resume soon, Moonvale was fucked.

"Don't look at me like that," I grumbled at Sookie. I could tell she was judging me. I bet she was just jealous that she was a cat and couldn't drink like us folk could.

She meowed at me, butting my ankle with her head.

"I know, I know, but you don't understand, Sookie. I *had* to have seven ciders. It was necessary."

She meowed again, this time quirking her head to the side.

"It's a long story. Weren't you there? Or did you sneak out before all the... exciting stuff happened?"

A throat cleared a few feet away.

In the midst of my conversation with Sookie, I hadn't noticed the door opening.

Redd stood stiffly by the front door, hovering at the threshold. "Hey, uh... I can't stay to help today; I'm working next door at the plant shop."

He'd come in just to tell me that? I stared at him for a minute. "Have fun?" I said questioningly.

"Fun, right. Yes. Well, I just wanted you to know," he explained awkwardly.

"You drop in and out all the time, that's just how it works. That's how it's always worked. You usually just do it and then tell me about it later." I crossed my arms and stared at him, perplexed.

His gaze dropped to my throat, and then jumped back up to my eyes. He inhaled deeply.

"Right. Just thought I'd be polite, since I was right next door anyways. Good day, Fiella." He turned to leave, pulling the door open.

"Wait." This was a bad idea. A *really* bad idea. But I couldn't stop myself. He froze instantly, his head whipping around to look at me.

I cleared my throat. "What are you doing this evening?"

He stared at me like I'd spoken gibberish.

"You know what? Neverm-"

"Yes."

"Pardon?" I asked, bewildered.

"Are you asking me out? My answer is yes. I owe you one after, you know... yesterday."

I stammered, "I– I wasn't asking you out!"

"Sure, you weren't." He smiled broadly, his fangs catching the lantern light. The force of his full smile was enough to knock the wind out of me. He had the kind of smile that would make any folk swoon. "Good day!" he called out.

He left before I could say anything else, leaving me feeling bewildered and a little flushed.

We didn't even agree on a time or a place, but I felt like I was floating in the clouds. I didn't even notice the hangover anymore.

"Don't look at me like that," I grumbled to Sookie after she was staring at me once again, but my reprimand had no bite to it. Sookie trilled in response, her tail swishing back and forth like she was up to no good.

The rest of the day passed in a blur.

I dropped a letter into the stone and mortar mailbox on the way home. The structure looked more stable than it had the last time I examined it–almost like someone had tried to subtly repair it. It was also radiating a slight warmth, melting the snow surrounding it. Strange.

I felt mildly guilty that I was going on a sort-of date with Redd instead of with my mysterious penpal. I wondered idly if my penpal would be upset at the idea of me going on a date. I tried to put myself in their boots, pondering if I would be upset if the situation was reversed. We were just friends, after all.

My thoughts were muddled. That was a problem I didn't want to worry about right now.

CHAPTER 28
Redd

I walked into Lunette's Plant shop, feeling lighter than I had in a long time.

I couldn't believe Fiella had asked me on a date. Well, she technically didn't, but she was going to.

Or... I had assumed she was going to. Maybe I just hoped that she was going to.

Regardless, I would be seeing the lovely vampire this evening and the thought brought a smile to my face.

That smile dropped as soon as I pushed open the door to Lunette's.

Oh, gods.

There was dirt everywhere. It seemed to be in every single nook and cranny, covering every visible surface. Even the walls were dusted with a fine layer of filth. It fluttered into the air as I walked by.

"Hello," I called out. "Lunette? Mayor Tommins sent me here to help with... your problem."

"Oh, hello!" shouted a voice from the back room. "One moment!"

I wasn't sure where to go, so I stayed put, trying to take a visual inventory of the room. It appeared that the largest problem was the dirt. Everything else looked relatively whole.

A tall, graceful druid woman came out from the back room. The smell of cherries wafted with her, and I found myself wishing for a berry smell instead.

I had seen her before, in the park and at the diner, but I had never spoken to the woman.

"Thank the gods! I was hoping to get some extra help around here today." She gestured around with dirty hands. "As you can see, I've got a bit of a mess."

I nodded. "I can certainly see that."

"Right. So, I'm not sure how much Tommins told you or how much you really care, but here's what happened," she stated. "I was bringing in my latest shipment of potting soil, but it must have frozen in its sack during the snowstorm, and somehow it burst as soon as I sat it down."

I didn't even want to know how that was possible. Sacks didn't usually burst, even with extreme temperatures. But that wasn't my business.

"Well, that is a problem. Sounds a little suspicious."

She sighed. "I know. It does. Regardless of the cause, I just need to get this cleaned up. If these plants don't get sunlight soon then they are going to wither–there is only so much my light enchantments can do."

Lunette handed me a pair of gloves, a few small sacks, and a small shovel, and nudged me toward the safe side of the shop to start working. I didn't want to know what she meant by safe–I just made sure not to wander too close to the area she was working in.

As I let my hands slip into the idle movements of scooping, gathering, and digging, my mind began to wander.

The worry crept in. I worried about my family back in Sunhaven. I worried about this town, and what I had done to it. I worried about the plants I was delicately shaking dirt from. I worried about Fiella, about her shop, about her delicate throat.

Things couldn't possibly stay this unfortunate forever. I kept hoping for a streak of good luck, but it didn't seem to be coming any time soon.

The hours dragged by, the excitement of my evening with Fiella making the minutes feel endless.

A black cat wandered in my direction, meowing at me and watching me curiously. The cats in this town were so *strange*. I didn't want to call them intimidating but something about the intensity of their gazes made me feel uneasy.

I had seen Fiella talk to her cat all the time, but it felt stupid to speak to a critter.

I cleared my throat hesitantly. "Um... Hello?"

The black cat hissed at me before scurrying away.

I looked around to make sure nobody had seen.

CHAPTER 29

Fiella

I was fluffing my hair in the mirror, admiring the blue tone, when I heard a knock on the front door. My heart immediately jumped to my throat. *He's here!*

"Come in! I'm just finishing getting ready!" I shouted as I tugged my most flattering sweater over my head. This sweater hugged my frame and made me look curvier than I was, and it matched my favorite boots *perfectly*.

The door opened slowly, and Redd tentatively stepped inside. "Hey, Fiella," he called out, shutting the door behind him and looking around. He didn't come any further than the entryway– he looked like he was afraid to take a single step. He clutched a slightly withered bouquet of flowers in his hands, his grip a bit too tight on the delicate stems.

"You can come all the way in, I swear nothing in here will bite. Except me." I tossed a wink in his direction and then remembered that I was going to apply my blood-infused lip gloss. I scurried back to my washroom.

He paused for a moment, and then I heard him take a

step. Then two. He began looking around. "Nice place," he commented. "It looks exactly how I expected it to."

I chose not to be offended by that comment. "Thanks! I did everything myself. Well, most of it. I'm almost ready, hang on."

I sprayed myself with my favorite fig and berry perfume, gave my hair one final fluff in the mirror, tucked the front strand behind my ear, and wandered out to the main area.

I caught a good look at Redd for the first time, my eyes dragging from his feet to the forget-me-nots in his grasp, all the way to his face. *Damn.* I had to discreetly wipe my chin to make sure I wasn't drooling. Redd looked incredible. The vampire was always infuriatingly handsome, but today, he looked even better.

His hair was tamed with product and his stubble was perfectly tidied. He was wearing trousers and clean boots, and a sweater that looked so soft that I wanted to rub my face on it.

I realized I was staring and shook myself out of it, only to realize that he was also staring at me. Thank the gods. I quirked my eyebrow at him and planted my hand on my hip.

"Ready, stranger? Or would you like to ogle me some more?"

He rolled his eyes at my use of his old nickname. "Don't make me regret this. Where should I put these?" He held the flowers out in my direction.

My heart squeezed at the gesture. *Forget-me-nots are my favorite.* I delicately pulled the bouquet from his grasp, ignoring the dusting of dirt coating some of the petals. I scampered to the kitchen to find a vase for them.

"Thank you! I can't believe you got me flowers! How'd you know to choose these ones?"

"I was working at Lunette's today, you know, and I might have mentioned something about seeing you later," he said a little bashfully.

I snorted. "Yep, that makes sense. How did you know where I live, by the way? Are you stalking me?"

"I only had to ask one person. This town is small, everyone knows where you live. Don't flatter yourself." He nudged me with his shoulder. I nudged him back twice as hard. Before he could get me back, I scampered ahead of him.

"Where to?" I asked.

"Well, there aren't many options, considering there are only two places in town that serve dinner and I don't feel like cooking today. How does Ginger's Pub sound? Some drinks, some food, some folk-watching?"

I smiled broadly, fangs poking my bottom lip. "Ginger's is perfect. Her stew is better than the diner's anyways, but don't tell anyone I said that."

"Your secrets are safe with me."

Redd cleared his throat. "You look incredible, by the way. You are always a beautiful woman, but you look especially lovely in that sweater."

I beamed at him, my cheeks burning hot. "Thank you. I was just thinking that you look rather ravishing yourself."

We hiked to Ginger's in companionable silence. I had my hands shoved into my cloak pockets because it was still *freezing* and covered in snow, but I made sure to accidentally (on purpose) brush shoulders with Redd a few times.

He even grasped my elbow to help me through some of

the especially deep snow patches, even though I was plenty tall enough to trek through them myself.

We passed an old mailbox on the way–the one that had started my journey with my penpal. I could almost swear that it was looking better than it had when I tripped over it a few weeks ago–the mortar less crumbled and the bricks more intact. But that didn't make any sense. Nobody maintained those things anymore.

It was now completely cleared of snow.

Redd caught me looking at the mailbox and asked, "Those things really are everywhere, huh? I wonder why nobody has knocked them down yet." He examined the stone structure with a curious scrutiny.

I shrugged, but I was secretly panicked at the thought of the mailboxes being taken down. I'd lose my penpal! "I guess it just feels right to leave them there. They're a fixture, you know? They've been there since the Old Gods roamed the realms. There would be no reason to take them down now."

"Yeah, maybe..." He murmured.

We slipped into Ginger's and chose a table near the back. It felt weird sitting here instead of my usual stool in the corner. The pub was especially crowded this evening. It was crowded every evening, but the snow must've been driving more people to drink than usual.

Understandable. Cheers to that.

Ginger flitted over to us and did a double take before she composed herself. "Fiella! Redd! Oh, how lovely to see you both. And together! Well, it's nice to see you anyways, but you know what I mean." She shook her head. "What can I get you guys?"

"Hi Ginger, I'll have today's cider with a shot of the best animal blood that's in the icebox right now, and whatever stew you've got boiling in the back today. And he'll have the same. Thanks!"

Redd tried to object but Ginger was already at the next table.

"Cider, huh? I guess that's... fine. I'm more of an ale guy myself."

"I knew you would be! I don't know how you drink that stuff. It tastes like piss." I shivered.

He quirked an eyebrow at me. "Now I don't know about you, but I don't typically drink piss, so I have no idea what you're talking about."

I sighed in exasperation. "Good one. Very funny."

He chuckled under his breath and glanced around. "I hope this stew is as good as you say it is. I've become a fan of the diner's dinners, that's where I've been eating most nights."

"Oh, trust me, it'll be the best thing you've ever tasted," I practically swooned. I caught a whiff of the stew on the way in. It smelled like today would be a fish grain tomato stew. Delicious.

Ginger returned and plopped the goblets and blood shots in front of us. I chose to down half of the shot and then pour the rest onto my goblet. Redd shrugged his shoulders and did the same. It seemed that he was resigned to following my lead today. I liked it.

"Okay, now ditch any preconceived ideas about ciders you had before this moment, and just try it." I was bouncing in excitement for him to try his first sip.

He glanced around nervously, seemed to realize that

time wouldn't stop if he indulged in a sweet drink instead of a pissy one, and let out a quiet sigh.

He lifted the goblet to his (admittedly very nice) lips and took a tentative sip. He hesitated, seemed to think for a moment, and then took another sip. He set the goblet down with a thunk and looked me in the eye.

"Fiella Elmwick. You were right and I was wrong. This is the second most delicious thing I've ever tasted." He had a mischievous glint in his eye.

I smiled so wide my cheeks hurt. "See! I told you so!" I took a sip of my own cider. Lavender blueberry. Yep, this flavor could win over any folk. "You said the second most delicious, what's been the most delicious? I'm curious." Tandor caught my eye across the pub and waved, a bright smile lighting up his face. I waved back.

Redd hadn't responded so I glanced back in his direction. He was staring at me pointedly, a slight flush to his cheeks. It took me a moment to understand what he was insinuating. I damn near choked on my cider. The thought sent a bolt of heat through me. I crossed my legs and tried not to squirm too obviously.

"*Oh*. Oh. Okay. Well," I didn't know what to say. I could feel the heat in my neck and my cheeks, I was sure I was as red as a tomato.

Redd laughed loudly, flashing his fangs. He so rarely laughed like that; it took my breath away. "You should see your face right now. I wish I could capture it in a painting." He took another swallow of cider, his throat working. "Sorry if that's rude, I'm just being honest. You are a delicacy." His tongue flicked out and caught a drip of cider before it could fall onto his perpetually stubbled chin.

I cleared my throat and willed the blood to leave my cheeks. "It's not rude at all, you just caught me by surprise." I took a gulp of my cider to calm myself. "I'm flattered, really. That's high praise."

"It is a *very* close second. This stuff is incredible."

I laughed and saw Ginger approaching from the corner of my eye. "Understandable. Just wait until you try the stew."

"Sweet talking my customers for me again, Fiella?" Ginger asked with a wink as she set our bowls in front of us. "I ought to pay you for that."

The heavenly scent of tomatoes and herbs hit my nose and I had to suppress a groan. "Keep feeding me these gods-blessed meals and I'll shout your praises from the rooftops. Thanks, Ginger."

"Enjoy! Shout if you need anything. I'll bring you another round of drinks after I finish making this lap." She twirled away with impressive speed, her hoofed feet clacking on the tiled floor.

The stew today was served with a few slices of warm sourdough bread. I ripped my bread to bits and tossed them into my bowl. Redd watched me with a pained expression on his face. "You're really going to mutilate a perfectly good slice of sourdough like that? Blasphemy."

"Don't knock it til you try it! You should know by now, I'm always right." I winked at him, blew on my spoonful to cool it down, and took a massive bite. The groan slipped out this time, I couldn't help it.

Redd cleared his throat and took a bite of his own stew. His eyes rolled into the back of his head for a moment before he seemed to come back to himself.

"I think I just had a religious experience," he said, immediately shoveling another spoonful into his mouth.

"Better than sex, right?" I joked.

"Now I don't know if I could go *that* far," he laughed, "but it's pretty gods damned close."

CHAPTER 30

Redd

I hated to admit it, but I was having more fun than I had had in months. Or possibly ever.

From the delicious drinks, to the life-changing food, to the effervescent laugh of the gorgeous vampire sitting next to me, this night was going to be a permanent fixture in my memories. I knew I would think back on this bright moment with fondness no matter where the fates took me in the future.

These were the things I would remember when I went back home to Sunhaven. The thought of returning home usually didn't stir up much emotion for me, but right now, it made me feel strangely... melancholy. That was a problem.

I tried to focus on staying in the moment and appreciating the day for what it was.

By the time we were on our third goblets of cider and second bowls of stew, I was feeling loose, uninhibited, and uncharacteristically happy.

I didn't want to ruin the mood by telling Fiella that I was returning home tomorrow.

Her face was flushed, her eyes were bright, and she was smiling more than I had ever seen her smile. She was positively radiant. I had a hard time pulling my eyes away from her.

I wondered if she would even notice my absence when I left—we were hardly even friends. We were just two vampires working together to fix her shop.

The thought made my smile droop. I couldn't get Fiella off my mind, but I couldn't stay here.

This town wasn't my home, even if I was growing to tolerate it.

I slapped a handful of silvers onto the table, sending my praises to Ginger. I would have written the faun a sonnet if I was a musical folk. Her culinary creations were *divine*. Absolutely Gods blessed.

"Thank you for the best meal of my life, Ginger, but we must be going." I called out. "If I have one more cider, I might never leave. You'll have to let me live behind the bar forever." I held my goblet over my head and let the final few drips fall into my mouth, savoring them like nectar.

"See! I told you her food was magical!" Fiella called out. "Ginny, looks like we've got another regular." She winked at the faun, and then winked at me. She looked so ridiculous that I couldn't help but smile.

Her words didn't even register past the warmth in my chest. I wouldn't get the chance to become a regular customer.

We donned our cloaks and headed out into the night.

"So," Fiella asked as we stepped up to the entry of her cottage. "Was that the absolute best meal that has ever graced your tongue or what? And the absolute best company too, I bet."

I simply smiled. My thoughts were bubbling and churning.

I couldn't fathom the idea of never kissing her, of never giving in to the urge to taste her lips with mine. If I was leaving tomorrow, this would be my only chance. I wasn't sure if I would be coming back.

Feeling emboldened by the buzz in my system and the rosy-cheeked smiles Fiella was showering me with, I decided *fuck it*. I grabbed her lovely chin, tilted her face up toward mine, and slowly, giving her plenty of time to pull away if she decided to, I lowered my mouth to hers. Delicate as a feather. Our lips brushed, barely a shadow of a touch. A shiver traveled down my spine.

Her gorgeous lips were even softer than I imagined they would be. She froze for a moment, and I almost decided to pull away and pretend the whole thing never happened, but then she reacted.

Fiella practically melted in my arms. She tasted like blueberries and something that was distinctly *her*, and I couldn't get enough. She pressed her lips harder against mine and threw her arms around my neck. I couldn't hold back the groan that slipped out of my mouth, the sound low enough to sound like a growl.

I moved my grip from her chin to cradle the back of her

head, and my other hand slipped to wrap around the small of her back, gently pulling her body into mine.

My blood was thrumming in my veins. I had never felt so alive. Fiella tightened her grip around my neck and tentatively opened her mouth, a question and an invitation.

Gods, this woman is going to be the death of me. I stroked my tongue against hers and she let out the sexiest rasp of breath I had ever heard. That sound was definitely going to be on repeat in my dreams.

I didn't even care that we were standing outside of her cottage and that it was freezing outside. I wanted this woman with every fiber of my being.

I nipped at her bottom lip with my fangs, not hard enough to draw blood but hard enough to sting a little, and Fiella let out a quiet laugh, a noticeable shiver moving down her spine.

"Tease," she rasped out against my mouth.

"What, would you like me to bite you again, Fiella?" I murmured back.

She groaned quietly in response, her nails digging into my skin and pulling me impossibly closer. "I didn't say that."

"You didn't deny it, either."

I scraped my fangs against her lip again, drawing the tiniest drop of blood, her delicious essence bursting on my tongue. This time, her moan couldn't be stifled, and I felt her knees weaken beneath her.

"You like that, don't you, little vampire?" I asked, unable to resist teasing her a bit.

She licked at my fang, surprising me and sending a shockwave of desire through my body. My heart was thrumming like a drum, my blood leaving my brain and heading to more *insistent* body parts instead.

"*Yes.*" She responded. She moved her hands down to my cloak, slipping them inside and tucking her body closer to mine, shoving the extra fabric out of the way.

I sent a silent thanks to the Old Gods, if any of them were lingering close enough to hear me. If I was struck dead at this exact moment with Fiella's lips on mine and her hands pulling me closer, I would die a happy man.

CHAPTER 31
Fiella

My mind was full of nothing but heat—mouths meeting, hands gripping, blood thrumming. I wanted more. I wanted everything. I wanted to drag him inside, yank his clothes off, and have my way with him.

Or let him have his way with me.

I blindly reached out with one hand, feeling for my doorknob. I wasn't willing to sacrifice a single moment of this scorching kiss.

Ah, got it. I yanked the door open, and we stumbled inside. As I glanced at the entry table to set my things down, I caught a glimpse of white paper.

Shit. I'd forgotten about my penpal. I suddenly felt like I was betraying my mysterious friend. Reality came crashing down like a tidal wave and I wrenched myself out of Redd's grasp.

"This is a bad idea. We shouldn't do this," I panted.

"What, why? What do you mean?" Redd looked bewildered, his face flushed, and his lips swollen. I purposely avoided looking down at the obvious bulge in his trousers.

He tried to reach for me again and I sidestepped away from his outstretched hand. He let it linger for a moment before he let it slowly drop to his side.

His eyes were glued to my face, trying to read my expression like a book. I locked my roiling emotions down so I could sort through them later.

"We just got carried away. Not a real date, remember?" I tried to laugh but it sounded more like a choke. My heart was still racing, and my body felt like lava.

He just looked confused. "Right... Okay Fiella. I'm sorry, you're right." He shook his head and ran his hands hastily through his mussed hair. "What you said. We just got carried away. I'll get out of your hair. Goodnight."

Redd fled my cottage and bee-lined back towards his end of town, hastily straightening out his clothes as he went.

Fuck. What have I gotten myself into? This was exactly the kind of mess I was trying to avoid.

I pulled the door shut, pressed my back into it, and slid to the floor, my face in my hands. My mind was spinning.

I could still feel the lingering heat of his hands on my skin, taste the blueberry and mint of him on my tongue, smell him in the air. I had to resist the urge to yank the door open, call out his name, and beg him to come back. Beg him to fill my mind so entirely that he was all I could think about.

I wanted him. I didn't just want to fuck him, and that was the problem. I wanted *all* of him. And that terrified me. I didn't want to give him the power to break my heart.

I didn't want him to take a part of me with him when he eventually left.

Redd didn't show up the next day.

Or the next day.

Or the day after that.

I didn't see him around town, either. We didn't cross paths in the square, he wasn't working in any of the neighbor's shops, and he didn't take any meals at the diner. He didn't walk back into Ginger's Pub for another taste of cider.

I had begun to accept that he had simply walked out of my life, that I had finally scared him away, that he had never intended to grow attached to me in the first place.

Maybe it was all in my head. He probably never really liked me anyways. He had been saying from the start that he didn't intend to stay in Moonvale forever–I knew this wasn't his home.

I just wished he would have said goodbye first.

His absence dug under my skin in a way I didn't expect it to. It needled between my muscles, through my bones, into my marrow. It ate at me in a way I couldn't shake.

Why hadn't he said goodbye?

I couldn't even write him a letter to find out, as I didn't know where he went. I supposed I could send a letter to his previous town in Sunhaven, but I had no way to know if he would be back there any time soon or if he was simply continuing his journey across the realm.

The dark cloud I had begun to escape settled back over my head, making everything seem just a bit greyer.

CHAPTER 32

Redd

My brain had become a bubbling cauldron.

I couldn't drag my mind away from worrying. Constant worrying. I dwelled on thoughts about my family, thoughts about this town, thoughts about a temperamental vampire.

Thoughts about a searing kiss that had ended too abruptly. Way too abruptly.

I kept analyzing my Ma's last letter over and over in my mind. It was so... wrong. Something about it was off. After tormenting myself for a few days, I couldn't take it anymore.

I wasn't proud of the way I had left home, and that small wound had festered over the weeks, growing and growing until it was an ache I could no longer ignore. Something needed to be done.

I let Mayor Tommins know that I had to leave, and that I didn't know when I'd be back. What I didn't tell him was that I also didn't know *if* I'd be coming back.

I gathered my meager belongings and set out on my

journey, leaving the key to my rental cottage tucked under a stone by the front door. If someone looked, they would eventually find it. I had paid enough silvers to the cottage owner that I had a few weeks to spare before they came seeking more payment or confirmed my absence.

I convinced myself that Fiella would be relieved to have me gone. Her strange rejection had left my mind reeling and my ego bruised. I didn't know what I did wrong. Everything had been going so well, we had been getting along so *perfectly*, and her body fit in my hands like it was made to be there.

I didn't know what had gone wrong.

All I knew was that I needed to get out of here. To get some space, and some clarity, and to finally set my mind at ease about what was going on back home in Sunhaven.

I felt a stab of regret that I hadn't told Fiella that I was leaving, but the desire not to bother her any more than I already had outweighed it.

The stables in Moonvale were pathetic. There was only one mule fit for the journey, and fit was an understatement. The stablemaster had explained that they would refill when tourists arrived with more critters, but for now, this was my only option beside traveling on foot.

I sighed as I handed over my silvers. This was going to be a long, miserable trip.

It had been weeks since I had been in the arid atmosphere of Sunhaven, and I had almost forgotten the way the air itself enveloped me in a warm cocoon.

Moonvale had surprisingly become familiar, and I was beginning to acclimate to the cold.

I was covered in a thin layer of sweat and uncomfortably warm. I loosened the laces of my tunic at my throat so I could let the air kiss my skin.

It seemed like nothing had changed in the weeks since I had left. The streets were as lively as ever, the sparse, stringy trees were as yellow as they had always been, the lizards scurrying across the path were zig zagging beneath my feet in the same patterns they always had.

My family's shop looked the exact same as well. It was still standing, the shingles on the roof still bright orange and hideous. I let out the breath I hadn't realized I'd been holding for what felt like weeks, the tension in my chest easing a fraction. I hadn't realized the fear that I had been holding onto was impacting me so deeply.

I had never been away from my family for longer than a few days, and the fact that they were able to carry on without me gave me mixed feelings. I was proud of them, but I was sad for myself. Maybe I wasn't so essential after all.

I strolled into the shop as though I had never left. It was the middle of the day, and I knew that some project would be in the works.

"Ma! Pa! It's me, Redd!" I called out as I entered, assuming one of my parents would be lingering in the vicinity as they usually did. The voice that answered me wasn't my parents, though–it was my younger brother Ollie.

"Redd? What in the Hell's Realm are you doing here!" he called out as he barreled around the corner and threw his body into my arms. I caught him with a grunt of effort and hugged him back. I had missed the casual affection of my family.

"I told you guys I wouldn't be gone forever," I grumbled into his fluffy head of hair. "I had to come back and visit. How are things? Where are Ma and Pa?"

Ollie extracted himself from my arms and looked into my face, examining me with an intensity I wasn't used to seeing in my lighthearted and free-spirited younger brother. He was barely considered an adult, and he often still acted like a little.

"They're back at home," he stated cautiously. He gnawed at his lower lip, his fangs almost pricking the skin. My hackles rose.

"They're workaholics, they're always in the shop at this time, why in the realms are they at home?" I asked suspiciously.

"Never mind that," he said hastily. "Let's talk about you! Where have you been all these weeks? Did you find a place to settle down? Do you have any fun stories? Meet any fun lads or ladies?" His excitement rose the longer he spoke.

I was surprised to find that I had actually missed the tornado of questions, and being the recipient again soothed something in me. The corner of my mouth lifted.

I settled myself onto one of the working stools as I braced myself to tell my brother everything that had transpired since I had left Sunhaven, and prepared for the interrogation I would be dropping onto him afterwards. I should have waited until we could gather the rest of the family, for I knew I would need to tell this tale more than once, but the eager glint in his gaze won me over.

My nose filled with the scent of cinnamon, clean linens, and the lingering tang of freshly baked sourdough as I walked into my parents' house. Home always smelled the same, and the scent settled my roiling nerves.

"Hey Ma, look who's here!" Ollie shouted as we walked inside and kicked off our boots. Ma never allowed outdoor shoes to be worn inside, that was blasphemous in her eyes.

My Ma entered the room carrying a basket of freshly folded laundry. All of Ma's grown littles had moved out years ago, but she still did our laundry every chance she got, claiming that none of us had the magic touch and that we would ruin the nice fabrics of our garments. I always thought that she secretly just liked taking care of us.

"Ollie? I thought you were on shop duty toda–" she broke off mid-sentence when she saw me in the entryway. She plopped the basket she was carrying onto the floor and yanked me into a warm hug. The top of her head didn't even reach my shoulder, and she wrapped her arms tightly around my waist, squeezing me with a strength that one wouldn't expect from a woman of her tiny stature.

"Redd! Honey, I'm thrilled to see you, but I told you we were doing just fine here, what in the realms are you doing back?" she chastised warmly. She refused to release me, clinging like a barnacle. I returned the hug, feeling my insides warm.

I had forgotten how much a good hug from Ma could brighten a day.

"I know, I know Ma, but you know I worry about you!

I scurried off so quickly and I wasn't sure how things would turn out here once I was gone." I tried to hide the relief in my voice. I didn't want her to know how much her vague letters had been eating at me in the weeks since I had left for Moonvale. I had been imagining the worst-case scenarios.

She leaned back and gripped me by the shoulders. "I told you things were fine, and I meant it, sweet foolish boy," she said warmly.

My Pa entered the room then. "What's all the fussing about in here?" he asked. "Ah, Redd! You're back! Good to see you, my boy!" He pulled me from Ma's grip and enveloped me in a hug of his own, thumping me firmly on the back in a way that would knock the breath out of a smaller folk.

His darkly bearded face was bright, and his cheeks were flushed, as though he had just finished a bout of belly laughter. He looked bright and full of life, a stark contrast to how sullen and defeated he had looked the last time I saw him. His one jagged fang caught the light as he smiled.

"We were just taking the day off to relax at home," he explained. "The boys have been handling the shop so well they hardly need our help anymore. I'm only really needed for special orders or projects that need more hands."

They proceeded to explain to me that things had gradually settled down, and that aside from the normal bouts of problems that arose in any folk's life, nothing out of the ordinary had been happening since around the time I had left. They had settled back into a peaceful routine, and even had the time to step back and enjoy the days for themselves.

The lingering tension in my muscles slowly drained away.

I settled into the sitting room with a cup of spearmint and gooseberry tea to reminisce with my family before dinner.

"You know, Ma, your letter really freaked me out. It didn't sound like you at all, and I could have sworn you purposely avoided answering my questions. Care to explain?" I grabbed a bowl of steamed pork and grains, heaping a pile onto my plate.

"Oh, honey, I was trying to multitask. You know how scatterbrained I can be. I just wanted to be sure you knew how much I missed you!" She reached over and patted the back of my hand that was resting on the table.

I let the relief of that wash over me, even as it irritated me a bit. I had gotten all worked up for nothing. They were perfectly fine, even having time for new hobbies and chores.

"So, you back for good? Did you scratch the exploring itch?" my Ma asked. "We can work you back into the rotation tomorrow, we've got a barn remodel to do over at the farm."

I had never really explained to my family why I had really left, merely mentioning the desire to travel. I was taken aback by the feeling that flooded me at the thought of never returning to Moonvale.

"Uh, no, I must go back at some point. They still need me," I explained lamely.

"We need you too, Redd," my Pa chimed in.

"Yeah, but you guys are clearly doing just fine here without me. And I left some of my clothes back at the cottage I was renting in Moonvale. I just need to go pick them up. And I promised the pub owner Ginger that I would build her a new set of high-top tables."

My Ma looked at me knowingly. She knew that clothes could easily be replaced, and that what I had rambled wasn't the real reason that I itched to return to the snowy town on the other side of the Barren Lands.

"Your clothes, huh?" she asked. "I didn't realize you were so attached to your belongings. Could there possibly be something else that is drawing you back to Moonvale?"

I fought the warmth that was spreading up my neck and into my face, willing my blood to be calm and still in my veins. I wasn't sure if it was working, and by the slight quirk to my Ma's mouth, I had a feeling it wasn't.

"I also told the mayor that I would be back. I can't betray his trust like that, he has been very consistent and helpful to me," I explained, not sure if I was digging my hole deeper or clawing my way out of it. The lie gnawed at me with tiny teeth.

"By the way you explained it, you've spent a good amount of your time with the owner of that trinket shop. It sounds like that was a huge project," she prodded.

I let out a deep sigh, knowing that it was no use trying to hide things from my Ma. She could read me like a book– she was exceptional at reading folk.

Keeping as much to myself as possible, I admitted that, perhaps, it wouldn't be the worst thing in the realms if I had to see the vivacious vampire running the trinket shop again. She was loud and obnoxious and achingly lovely, but she was surprisingly pleasant to be around.

Her energy had begun to seep between the cracks in my

defenses, and she was slowly crawling under my skin, inch by inch. I wasn't sure if I would be able to get her out again. She had breached my defenses in a way no other had before.

And, technically, the shop wasn't finished yet. She could use more of my help.

"Oooooh, Redd's got a crush!" my brother Ollie chimed in a singsong voice.

"I'm a grown ass man. It's not a *crush*," I defended. "I just think she's a very impressive and admirable woman. She works hard. She takes no bullshit. She speaks her mind."

"*Impressive and admirable?* Forget a crush, Redd's in love," my brother Wayde mocked.

"You've been with your lady since you were littles, you shouldn't be offering romantic feedback to anyone," I grumbled, glaring at him, uncomfortable with the turn the conversation had taken. My family was big on mocking–anything and everything was fair game with us, but for some reason I found myself wanting to protect the idea of Fiella and keep her to myself.

I wanted to wrap her stories up inside myself and shelter them from the realms, where they were mine alone and I didn't have to share them.

I wanted the bits and pieces of her to be mine.

I wanted her to be mine.

CHAPTER 33
Fiella

Kizzi dragged me into the park to meet with the other local witches—some of whom I knew personally, some of whom I had only met on occasion, and a few of whom I had never seen before. They must have traveled here for the occasion.

I tried to set my sulking aside to focus, but I was struggling. My mind kept trying to wander.

Kizzi cleared her throat to bring the focus onto herself. "Ladies, I know we've been working on the hush hush for the past few days, but I think it's time we finally let Fiella know exactly what has been going on."

"Wait a second. What is going on?" I asked, confused.

Kizzi patted the back of my hand. "It's alright Fi, just breathe for a sec, we'll fill you in. I told you I would get to the bottom of this, and I think I have. Or at least part of it. We'll explain."

She gestured to one of the other witches in the group, a strong and imposing woman with fire red hair cropped close to her chin. She introduced herself to me as Gertrude.

"Miss Fiella, as I'm sure you are aware, there has been a string of unfortunate... incidents that have been occurring in Moonvale. Your shop's beetle infestation. The increased illnesses. Sprites running amok. The damaged buildings throughout town. Et cetera. As I'm sure you are also aware, given the circumstances you yourself were in, most of these incidents seem to be magical in nature," she explained. "Now, magic doesn't cause mischief on its own. While it isn't sentient, magic tends to err towards causing peace and order, not mischief and strife. Something dark is at play here."

My mind was whirling with the overload of information. "Okay," I said slowly. "Something dark? Like dark magic, dark sorcery? How does that even work?"

Gertrude patiently explained further. "The magic of the Old Gods is naturally light, but with evil intentions and a lot of time and effort, stubborn folk can twist it to become something ugly. We think this is the case here."

"Who the fuck would do that?" I asked.

Gertrude startled at my use of profanity, but quickly composed herself and delicately cleared her throat. "That's what we need your help to figure out. We have been following magical trails and tracing magical signatures, and it seems as though your beetles have come from a town called Willowvalley. Have you been there, or do you know anyone from there?" she asked.

"Willowvalley... I haven't been there in ages. It's one of the towns my family sources trinkets from. Sure, we travel all over the realm, but I don't think anything very significant comes to mind. I certainly don't remember a group of evil folk there..." I drifted off as I sank deeper into thought, trying to pull out any crumbs that could be helpful.

There was that bartender who refused to serve more than one alcoholic drink to any women folk, but I think he was just an asshole, not an evil magic wielder. There were a few littles who attempted to steal my rental horse. Just the usual nonsense, nothing that jumped out as dark magic.

My attention was pulled back to the group when Kizzi's voice rang out above the chatter of the others. "Well, you all know what that means."

Ten pairs of eyes stared at her expectantly, clearly not knowing what that meant.

She rolled her eyes dramatically. "We're going to Willowvalley to dig up this rotten egg! Duh!"

I let that sink in. Well, I certainly would love the chance to figure out who destroyed my shop and spit in their face the way they deserved.

"Okay, sure," I agreed. I didn't have anything better to do at the moment.

"Great! Let's take off at first light. I've got some things to pack and some favors to call in, but I just know we're going to catch this son of a bitch."

I wasn't as certain as she was, but I would seize the opportunity that presented itself. We were not sure if this perpetrator was one folk, or one hundred folk, or if this act was connected to the rest of the mischievous situations in Moonvale. It was all so mysterious.

Gertrude mentioned many magical signatures and many magical trails... but this was somewhere to start, and I latched onto it.

I would avenge my losses.

<h1 style="text-align:center">CHAPTER 34
Redd</h1>

I stayed in Sunhaven for a few more days, sinking seamlessly back into my previous patterns, except for the fact that I was in my parents' spare room instead of my personal flat. I woke up, took some thirst tonic (that *wouldn't* cause any mysterious side effects, thank the gods), brewed myself a latte, and headed to the shop to complete the day's work.

I was surprised to find that I felt... bored. In all my years living in Sunhaven and the countless hours I had spent working in the shop, I had never felt myself itching for something more. For some chaos. For unexpected challenges. For turns in my plan that would force me to improvise and think on my feet.

For curses that would require goofy magical rituals. For folk that would worm their way under my armor and into my heart.

I realized that, unfortunately, I missed Moonvale. I missed the way the entire town seemed determined to speak to me, no matter what unapproachable expression was on my face. I missed the old, crumbly mailbox on the corner that had introduced me to my penpal. I missed having to bundle up into as many layers as possible, because even though the outside was miserably cold, the relief of finally making it to the warm and cozy destination was so unexpectedly sweet. I missed the fluffy critters that scurried up the trees and peacefully munched on their treats. I missed the stew in the diner, and I missed lavender blueberry ciders.

I missed the gorgeous vampire that I couldn't seem to pry from my thoughts.

I missed Fiella. I wanted to be around Fiella.

I couldn't help but ache for her. Yearn for her. Gravitate towards her. Everything about her pulled me in. I replayed our kiss on loop, her lips constantly on my mind.

Moonvale wasn't my home. I didn't belong there. Fiella rejected me. She didn't want me, but I couldn't help but imagine what would happen if she did.

Oh gods, I'm fucked.

~

My Pa approached me in the shop, casually sitting down at the workstation next to me and plopping a segment of oak log onto the counter.

"Hey, bud. I remember you mentioned that that lady friend of yours works at a trinket shop and that most of her wares were destroyed," he stated nonchalantly, pulling out a chisel and a knife to begin his woodworking.

"Hey Pa. That's right," I responded, dusting the wood

shavings off of my lap and turning his way. "She was really upset about it–she worked hard on that shop."

It looked like he was setting up to begin one of his notorious carvings. He was renowned for his intricate wooden sculptures. He could create just about anything, but his favorite thing to create was different folk. Vampires, humans, sirens–the man was an artist and could create anything. He could also create critters that were so lifelike, you swore they would scurry right off of the counter.

"I've got a few pieces that have been sitting around collecting dust, why don't you bring her some of them? I've been meaning to get rid of them, anyway."

I stared at him, unable to contain my surprise. I had considered helping Fiella with her restocking situation, but I didn't know how to approach the subject without crossing any boundaries. I knew how much thought and care she had put into procuring her shop items, and how she had spent years painstakingly pulling the collection together. She was particular about her shop's offerings.

But she was practically starting from scratch at this point, and everyone could use a little help from time to time. And I had seen a few damaged animal sculptures in the wreckage during my days of cleaning, so I already knew she would love them.

"That's actually a great idea, Pa," I answered warmly. "Thank you. I'm sure she would love to offer your masterpieces in her shop. The folk of Moonvale will be fighting over them."

He grunted and flopped his hand in the air to brush my statement off, but when he got back to work, I was sure that I saw the ghost of a smile on his mouth.

We worked in a companionable quiet for the rest of the day, only speaking up occasionally. He completed an exquisite sculpture of a water faerie, while I finished cutting and measuring all the boards that would be required to redo the hull of a riverboat.

The idle companionship was comforting, in an old and repetitive sort of way, but I couldn't help but notice that it didn't invigorate me in the way Fiella's idle chatter did.

I was in way over my head, and if I didn't figure this out soon, I feared that I would drown.

I packed up my mule and saddlebag to leave, bracing for yet another trek through the Barren Lands. The hardy steeds of the hot regions could handle the journey easily, and they could even handle much worse, but I felt guilty sending them through it, nonetheless.

There were rumors about how the Barren Lands had once been a thriving oasis, full of unique critters and the most beautiful scenic foliage in the whole realm. That otherworldly beauty could only come from magic. When the Old Gods abandoned the realms so many lifetimes ago, they had stripped the soul of the oasis, leaving us with the desolate and deadly landscape that so few could traverse today.

The mule and I would've appreciated a more hospitable journey.

I couldn't stop my mind from wandering back to Moonvale, wondering what had occurred there in the time I had been away.

I was itching to send off the letter I had penned right before leaving Sunhaven. It was burning a hole in my pocket. I had decided that I wanted to figure out who my mysterious writing companion was.

My thoughts were conflicted. I was finding myself drawn toward Fiella, but I couldn't deny the connection I had with the mystery folk either. What I had with Fiella right now wasn't solid, it wasn't tangible, and it could have possibly been all in my head. For all I knew, the vampire had found a new companion while I had been away.

I needed answers.

CHAPTER 35
Fiella

"You know what, I'm just going to say it. This place sucks ass," Kizzi declared, thunking her goblet onto the sticky counter.

Her green hair was damp with sweat and curling around her pointed ears. I was sure mine looked much worse.

We had used some of Kizzi's (very expensive) magic reserve to spell some enchanted doves to carry us to Willow-valley, and we were not thrilled about it.

The snows had cleared up, thanks to the hard work of the witches, and the weather was becoming mild enough to soon allow travel. That didn't mean our journey had been pleasant, though. Quite the opposite. Air travel always made me queasy, and the oversized magical birds were downright beastly.

We were sitting in a tavern that was a hovel compared to Ginger's cozy set up. It was crowded and grimy and smelled more like sweaty bodies than it did like ale and stew.

The cider I sipped on was dull and flat. It tasted like it

had been watered down. I swallowed it anyway, hoping it would settle my frazzled nerves.

We were here on a mission, staking a lookout to see if anyone appeared to be a wielder of dark sorcery. We didn't really know what dark sorcery *looked* like, or if it was distinguishable on the wielder at all, but we were hoping for some sort of sign. Maybe they had tar tipped fingers.

A gritty voice behind me caused my muscles to tighten, goosebumps raising on my skin. I held down a disgusted shiver.

"Well, well, well, if it isn't my sweeeeeeet Fiiiiiiiiiiiella," the man slurred out, his hot breath steaming in my ear. I fought the urge to whirl around and punch him–I couldn't afford to end up in any dungeons today.

A clammy, heavy hand landed on my shoulder, nails digging into my tunic. I whipped around and held my fork to the man's throat, threatening to skewer his jugular with it. It wasn't as effective as a knife, but it would do the trick with enough force. I wasn't getting my fangs anywhere *near* this vermin.

"Get your disgusting hands off of me, you prick," I snarled.

He was so startled that he nearly fell on his ass, wobbling for a few second before he righted himself again. "Hells Realm! Fuck! I was just saying hello!" he stammered.

I recognized him a moment later, the memories of him clicking into place.

"You've got to be fucking kidding me." I pulled the fork away from his exposed flesh. "Josten?"

"I knew you would come find me eventually, baby." A weasley smile crawled across his face. "I've been waiting for you."

I was flabbergasted. I hadn't seen this miserable wizard in *years*. What did he mean, waiting for me?

Kizzi took that moment to step in. "Um, excuse me asshole, please sit the fuck down. Nope, over there, thank you," she instructed, making him sit at the next table over instead of right by us.

Josten fell into a chair, that nasty smile still plastered on his face.

"I knew it would work; I knew it! I knew it. Ha ha ha," he babbled.

Kizzi slapped her hands onto the table with a crack. Josten jumped.

"What in the realms are you talking about, asshole?" she asked.

"It took a while; I was expecting you weeks ago. You're very stubborn. And very hard to find. Did you like my gifts? Which one was your favorite?" the wizard asked.

"Gifts?" I asked, astonished. "What gifts? Are you on drugs? Is it the mirthroot again?"

"I've been sending them your way for months! Well, years, really. But I've been trying harder the past few months. You move around a lot, you're a hard vampire to track."

"Again, I ask, what the fuck?"

Kizzi pulled a pouch from her pocket and dumped the

powder into her palm. She leaned toward Josten and blew it into his face. He sputtered, but his gaze focused on Kizzi immediately.

"What in Hell's Realm, lady?" he asked, wiping his face frantically, clawing the powder residue out of his eyes.

Kizzi waved her hand dismissively. "Oh, calm down, it's just a little mixture to sharpen your senses. Sober you up a bit. It's not poison or anything." Kizzi hesitated, then picked up her pouch, inspecting the remaining contents. "I hope."

Josten stared at Kizzi with fear, his eyes as wide as saucers.

I chugged the rest of my watery cider and then spoke up, interrupting the lovely moment. "Alright Josten, I think it's time you explain yourself."

It took him a few heartbeats, but he seemed to be more clear-headed. The manic gleam in his eyes was still present, but the drunken sheen had cleared, at least enough for him to speak.

"Wouldn't you rather take this somewhere more private? I've missed you."

"Absolutely the fuck not. Now you better explain what gifts you are referring to before I shove this thing where it doesn't belong," I threatened, twirling the fork between my fingers.

He gulped. "Okay fine. Gods, I forgot how angry you are. I thought you would have gotten kinder over the years." He set his hands on the table, leaning forward.

I smiled, flashing my deadly fangs. "I wouldn't dare."

He shuddered. "Right. Okay. Well, the truth is, I miss

you, Fi. I can't stand the thought of you out there, alone, without me."

In a flash, I stabbed the fork into the tender flesh between his thumb and forefinger. I removed it before anyone could see me, but not before he let out a pitiful howl of pain. I didn't even draw that much blood, only a few drops. The scent that bloomed in the air was putrid.

"You lost the right to call me Fi ages ago, and you know that. Remember your place, asshole."

The folk that glanced our way quickly found more entertaining things to watch in the crowded tavern, the noise barely audible over the other voices and the bard playing tunes in the corner.

I held the fork up threateningly.

"Fine! Fine, gods just give me one minute." The vile man was oozing sweat, his pulse thudding visibly under his skin. Gross.

"I've been thinking about you lately, so I've been using some tracking spells to see where you've been going. But gods, you move around a lot! Never in the same place for long! I've been sending you signals for ages, but you usually move along by the time they land. You're a tough lady to track down!"

"Signals? What does that mean? Why didn't you just send me a letter like a normal person?"

Kizzi coughed. "Eh, that would be on me, actually. Well, me and the rest of the witches. We placed a spell on the town so none of his missives could make it to you."

At my bewildered look, Kizzi explained further. "It's just that you were so sad when he cheated on you! And he was such a piece of shit! And I wanted you to protect your peace and–"

I cut her off with a hand on her arm. "Kiz, moons, I'm not mad at you! Don't get yourself worked up."

She visibly exhaled. "I know I should've spoken to you about it first, but I didn't even want to say his grimy name out loud." She shuddered dramatically.

I wasn't the biggest fan of Josten. Well, honestly, I would scoop his eyeballs out with a spoon and feed them to the critters if I could, but I didn't dwell on it. Anymore. He had already taken enough from me, so I refused to let him take anything else.

Then it finally clicked. I turned towards him. Slowly. Gritting my teeth with enough force to crack stone.

"You..."

He gulped. "Just let me explain more, baby! I was trying to–"

I lunged at him before he could get another word out, my fingernails seeking the skin of his throat.

"You absolute fucking monster! You piece of dirt! You garbage mole! You–"

Kizzi stopped me before I could inflict any more damage, saving me from a night in the dungeons while I vibrated in fury.

"You sent the fucking beetles."

"They were supposed to spell out a message! Did you get it? *Josten luvs Fiella?*"

"Spell out a message?! Those things ate my shop! Destroyed it! Everything I've worked for!" I had to stop myself from tearing free from Kizzi's grasp.

He visibly paled. "Woahhhhhh. They weren't supposed to do all that."

"What did you expect, dealing with dark magic? That stuff is uncontrollable!!" Kizzi shouted.

"But the other messages..." I didn't think it was possible, but his pasty complexion became even more ghost-like.

"They've all gone wrong, you idiot! You've been terrorizing the entire town! Making an absolute mess!!" I thundered.

Kizzi chimed in. "Dark magic spirals, you gods damned idiot. Once you send it off, it never does what you wanted it to do. You've even been screwing with other towns!"

"I mean, those Moonvale losers probably deserved it," he grumbled.

"And the other towns? Sunhaven? Did you send any *messages* there as well?"

"Well... You spent some time there, during the freeze season, I thought you might have moved there. I may have convinced the coven to help me out, we've been tracking you for seasons. You've been to many towns, so we've sent many... messages."

"And the snowstorm? Was that you too?"

"I was hoping a little bit of a chill would encourage you to come here to Willowvalley..."

"Alright, I've had enough of this dirtball. Let's get him taken care of," I declared.

"I was hoping you'd say that," Kizzi responded with a mischievous smile.

"Wait! Wait, stop! What are you doing! No!" He struggled violently, but the alcohol was still slowing his reflexes down even though Kizzi's concoction had cleared his mind. He was an easy target.

His kicking and screaming and begging for mercy was even sweeter than I thought it would be.

As soon as we got him outside, I spit in his face, right on his forehead, like I promised myself that I would.

It was spectacular.

Kizzi and I dragged Josten to the Willowvalley dungeon while he screamed and cried like a baby.

CHAPTER 36
Redd

The crisp air of Moonvale greeted me like an old friend, wrapping around my face and slipping under my flowing cloak with cold, but comforting tendrils. I felt lighter than I had in days. This was *right*.

Before I even dropped my bags off at my rental cottage, I went straight to Fiella's Finds. I was regretting not speaking to Fiella before I had left, and I was afraid of what I would encounter.

Would she turn me away? Would she have someone new here? Would she be happy to see me? Would she even care?

The questions rattled around in my brain as I walked briskly to the trinket shop, dodging the attempts at conversation from the folk I passed. I was excited to see Fiella's lovely face when I gave her the sculptures my Pa had made for her.

When I reached my destination, I was disappointed to find the front door locked. A glance in the windows told me the lamps were dark. The place was empty.

A bump against my ankle startled me into jumping. My heartbeat spiked.

"Meooow!"

"Fuck!"

Just Sookie. That gods damned cat.

With a sigh, I bent down to scratch her chin. "Hi there, you strange cat. Where is your mom?"

Sookie let out a trill, bumping her head against my hand.

"She's not here, is she? Is she at Kizzi's?"

The cat stepped back and looked at me blankly, her eyes trying to tell me something that I couldn't decipher.

"Okay… Not Kizzi's, I'm assuming. Is she in her cottage? Sleeping, maybe?"

The cat continued to stare at me, her tail swishing behind her. Somehow her gaze felt… condescending.

I stopped to consider that I was having a conversation with a cat, and that perhaps I had finally lost my mind. The critter had such intelligence in her gaze that it was easy to forget that she wasn't another folk.

I tried one last time. "Can you show me where she is?"

At this, Sookie turned and took off running. Ignoring the strangeness of the situation, I followed. I only made it a few paces before I lost sight of the critter around the corner. *Gods, that little lady is quick.* Impossibly, she was much faster than my vampire speed.

The cat had disappeared like a wraith, leaving me in the midst of the town square with more questions than answers. I let out a deep sigh, the air coming all the way from my toes.

Feeling a little foolish and discouraged, I decided to

freshen up at my rental cottage before continuing my search. I discreetly sniffed at my collar. A bath certainly wouldn't hurt.

Perhaps Fiella was with Kizzi somewhere or taking a meal break. I was sure I would find her soon enough.

I owed a visit to Mayor Tommins as well. My long day just became even longer. It seemed I owed everyone in this town an apology or two.

CHAPTER 37
Fiella

I felt as light as air when I woke up the next morning in my own bed, the dark cloud unable to settle over me.

I had finally figured out who had destroyed my shop, and while that didn't undo any of the damage or erase any of the lingering pain I still felt, it did make me feel more settled. At peace with the situation.

The mayor of Willowvalley had been thrilled when Kizzi and I dropped Josten off at his dungeon. Apparently, he had received many reports about various magical mishaps, but he didn't have enough proof from the local townsfolk.

We provided enough evidence to have Josten locked up for a *long* time, and for his sorcery magic to be stripped. Good riddance.

The distraction had been enough to pull my thoughts away from Redd. At least temporarily.

The handsome vampire always crawled back into my mind, no matter how hard I tried to keep him out of it.

As I swept the seemingly endless dust into the corner of

my shop, I considered the vast empty shelves that now lined the walls. While most of the wreckage and damage had been repaired, and my new shelving was beautiful, it looked sparse without my beloved collection of knick knacks.

I had brought home a few pieces from Willowvalley–a few sets of teacups and goblets, a painted vase, and a lovely lamp–but it wasn't nearly enough. Not even close.

The measly supply I had would only make me a handful of silvers in sales. It wouldn't even come close to covering the debt I had accrued for the supplies to fix my shop.

I needed to travel. I needed to restock. And I needed to do it soon.

~

The day crawled by at a snail's pace. The shop felt empty. Cold even though a fire was crackling in the newly installed hearth.

I was working in the unfinished loft, having climbed the half-built stairs more like a ladder. The new daybed I had just hauled up looked lonely without any storage crates surrounding it.

I had finished off the last of Kizzi's bluebell-infused thirst tonic before our journey, so I made a mental note to pick up another. My blue hair, twisted into a messy knot on my head, had grown on me. I was strangely sad to think about my strands fading back into a caramel color. Maybe Kizzi could help me keep it around...

I was pulled from my musings by the sound of my front

door opening and the bell chiming. Paw pads pattered in my direction, deftly climbing the unfinished stairs.

"Meow!" Sookie called out, followed by a chunky orange cat.

How she managed to open the front door, I did not know. I chose not to consider the conundrum too closely.

"My baby girl! I've missed you!" I called out, bending down to scratch her chin. "Who's your friend here?" I stuck my hand out for the orange cat, but he merely sniffed my hand and moved along. Rude, but understandable. I didn't like strangers either.

Sookie soaked up my attention for long minutes, making up for lost time. "I bet you missed me, huh. Did you manage to steal any pastry crumbs while I was gone?" I cooed.

She purred in response.

The front door opened again, the breeze carrying in the familiar scent of mint and sandalwood that I didn't think I would ever smell again. A swarm of butterflies erupted in my stomach, fluttering and trying to break free. My heart took off at a gallop.

"Why, the stranger has returned," I called out, keeping my eyes on the cat in front of me even though they ached to take in the vampire. I tried to keep my voice from betraying the roiling emotions I felt.

"Hello to you too, sweet Fiella," Redd said, his voice rough around the edges. He stepped in and closed the door. He took one step towards me.

Two.

Three.

He approached the stairs to the loft, and he came into view as he climbed up to the upper level with me.

I rose slowly, finally glancing in his direction.

It was like a punch to the gut. I had forgotten how handsome Redd was, and his face was pulled into a tentative smile. Nervous. Perhaps... bashful?

I had been so distracted by his face that it took me a few heartbeats to notice what was in his arms. His sleeves were rolled up past his elbows, and his muscles were taut under the weight of the basket.

My jaw went slack at what I saw. I flew to his side, mesmerized. The basket was carrying the most beautiful creations I had ever seen. Sculptures, of both critters and folk, carved with the precision only a master could manage. I reached out a finger, desperate to find out if they were real or just a mirage of perfection.

Redd's deep chuckle distracted me. "Why Fiella, it is alarming to see you so speechless. Shall I call Velline? Do you need a medic?"

I flushed all the way to my hairline. I wasn't sure if I was more embarrassed to be caught staring at him or at his sculptures.

I cleared my throat, trying to regain my cool. "Who, me? I could never be speechless. What do you have there?"

"Isn't there another question you'd rather ask first?" he asked, quirking a full eyebrow. "I was expecting you to scream at me. Perhaps throw a few things. At least grant me one of those adorable glares."

I snorted, with only a dash of humor, "Oh right. Where in the Hell's Realm have you been? You vanished like a wraith. I didn't think I'd ever see you again."

"You can't get rid of me that easily, sweet Fiella." He smiled for just a moment, and then it dropped from his face. "I had something to take care of back in Sunhaven. I'm sorry I didn't tell you first, I just... After that night..."

"You don't owe me anything. It's fine, Redd."

"No. It's not fine. I should have told you I was leaving but I was afraid that if I had to look into your eyes, I wouldn't be able to go."

He set the basket down on a nearby shelf and turned back to face me. He reached out slowly, giving me time to pull away if I chose to, and grasped my shoulders. My breath caught in my throat at the look on his face–pained, eager, *pleading*.

He slowly lowered his face toward mine, his brown eyes glowing in the fire light.

Holy shit, is he going to kiss me? Do I want *him to kiss me?* My body acted without my permission, my face tilting up like a flower reaching for sunlight.

I could feel his pulse thumping in his veins almost as hard as mine, our hearts echoes of each other. He hesitated for a heartbeat before his eyes closed. Mine followed.

Instead of softly pressing his lips against mine, he leaned our foreheads together.

I tried to contain my disappointment. I was supposed to be mad at him for leaving without warning, not aching for him to kiss me.

I scrunched my eyes shut even tighter. His warm breath caressed my face. His hands slid from my shoulders, over my neck, to the base of my skull, cradling my head.

We stayed there for long heartbeats, sharing breath, neither of us willing to shatter the fragile moment.

He exhaled heavily before he spoke. "I am going to speak, and I would like you to listen to everything before you respond."

His scent was hypnotizing me. Lulling my senses. His grip on my head kept me solid.

"What do you mean? What if I hav–"

"Fiella," he interrupted me. "Please."

With a sigh, I agreed.

"You already know the story about why I left Sunhaven, but that isn't what I told my family when I departed. I just fled as quickly as I could," he stated. "I knew I had to go back. To check on them. To make sure they were okay. My Ma had sent me a few letters, but they were strange." He shook his head. "I was already planning to go, but then you asked me out."

"I didn't! I–"

"Fiella," he chastised me.

"Sorry. Continue."

"There was never the right moment to tell you. And then we kissed, and then you slammed the door in my face, and... I just left." He sighed, caressing the back of my head with slow strokes of his fingers. "For a moment, just a moment, I considered never coming back."

I tried to object but he pressed his thumb over my mouth, silencing me. "I know. I know, Fiella. But I couldn't. Did you hear that? Let me say it again so you understand me completely. I couldn't stay away from you. The thought of never seeing your face again, never hearing your laugh, never..." He shook his head lightly, as though clearing those thoughts away. "I couldn't take it. It made me *sick*."

His thumb rubbed over my bottom lip, gently, back and forth. A shiver crawled down my spine.

"I had to come back. I wouldn't have been able to live with myself if I let you go without telling you how I feel. Without taking a chance. Because even if you take my heart and stomp all over it, I had to at least *try*."

He released me and stepped back, finally meeting my gaze. My skin felt cold without his warmth.

I knew what the action meant. He was giving me a moment to think, to process, to breathe. But he didn't go far.

The space between us was small, but it contained the whole realm.

"So, what do you say, my sweet Fiella? What will it be?"

I found myself speechless once again.

CHAPTER 38
Fiella

I stared into Redd's eyes, getting lost in the deep hue that seemed to swallow me whole. I could reach out and touch him if I was brave enough to. I could close the gap between us in an instant.

He stared back at me, a man ruined, his entire soul bared on his face.

This moment would change everything, and we both knew it. What happened next would decide our fates.

The moment lingered, neither of us willing to take the leap and risk the outcome. My heart pounded in my ears, a flush crawling up my cheeks at his proximity.

I could sense his blood pumping under his skin, his flesh begging to be licked, to be bitten.

He leaned toward me infinitesimally, the gap between us shrinking. His lips hovered only a few inches from mine.

I inhaled, pulling air deep into my lungs. His mint and sandalwood scent enveloped me, soothing my jagged nerves and overwhelming my senses.

I used every ounce of willpower I had to keep my feet

planted, to keep myself from drifting forward. The fear kept me rooted in place.

His tongue darted across his lips, and my eyes flicked to the movement. The flush crawled past my cheeks and into my ears, my skin burning. I was on fire.

He noticed my gaze, and he exhaled heavily.

"Fiella..." His voice was a prayer. A curse. An omen.

My eyes flitted back up to his.

Slowly, so slowly he stepped forward, the step taking minutes. Hours. Years. I stayed frozen, holding my breath. He closed the gap between us, his eyes holding a million questions. I could feel his warmth radiating, only a breath between us.

I had forgotten how tall he was, but this close, I had to crane my neck to keep eye contact. His head was bent down, our faces drawn together like magnets.

His hand came next. He raised it slowly, giving me plenty of time to step away from it if I wanted to.

I didn't.

His palm cupped my jaw, as delicate as a butterfly's wing, barely making contact. A question. An offering. A promise.

After only a moment's hesitation, I leaned into his touch, relishing in the feeling of his rough skin against mine. An acceptance. A truth. A blessing.

He reacted instantly, his grip tightening on my jaw and his other hand coming up to clutch my face.

"Thank the gods," he murmured, before slamming his lips to mine.

He didn't hold back, pouring himself into the kiss. I

matched his fervor, gripping his tunic in my fists, yanking him towards me, pressing our bodies together.

Yes. This is right. This is everything.

He kissed me like he had nothing to lose, his mouth devouring mine. My blood thrummed, my fangs deliciously aching.

After realm-quaking minutes, his mouth left mine, my body liquid in hands. I panted, unable to catch my breath. His mouth moved to my throat, kissing, licking, fangs scraping. An indecent moan escaped my mouth.

He shivered. "Gods Fiella, you make the most delicious sounds." His fangs scraped me again–a promise and a taunt.

"Keep doing that. Please. Fuck, Redd. Sink your fangs into me," I begged.

A low laugh rumbled through his chest. "You have no idea how badly I ache for the taste of you. For your blood in my mouth, your essence on my tongue. But not yet, my sweet Fiella." His mouth moved to my collarbone. "Not yet."

I shivered, grabbing onto his chest, my fingers finding the laces of his tunic.

"Tease," I complained.

"Don't worry, little vampire, I would never leave you aching. Be a good girl and be patient."

His words lit my blood on fire, arousal settling deep into my stomach, my core clenching.

"Is that a promise?" I asked breathlessly. I managed to loosen his tunic, sliding my hands beneath to get to his skin beneath. I needed *more*.

He didn't respond, but I could feel his smile against my skin.

"Are you trying to get me naked, little vampire?" he asked when my hands continued the exploration of his torso.

"Yes. Of course. Please," I answered, my mind whirling.

"So polite, how could I say no?" he said wryly. He stepped back just far enough to whip his tunic off. I could feel his eyes on my face, watching me watch him as he stripped for me. So slowly. Too slowly. His hands paused at the button on his trousers, and I frowned in protest.

"Your turn."

I flushed, the blood pounding under my skin almost painful.

I didn't hesitate, wanting him to see me, wanting him to have *all* of me. I pulled my sweater over my head.

His sharp intake of breath was the most satisfying sound I had ever heard, and any worry about him not liking my appearance disappeared in an instant. I could tell by his face that he was enraptured. Hypnotized.

"I swear, Fiella, you were carved by the Old Gods themselves. You are the most stunning creature I have ever seen. I could look at you every day, every hour, every minute for the rest of my life and never get used of the sight," he murmured, his eyes feasting on my flesh, raking over every exposed inch of me. My nipples tightened in the cool air.

"You aren't too bad to look at yourself," I panted. "Have you ever considered having an artist paint you? Folk would pay good silvers to look at all *this* every day."

He choked. "I'd consider it, but only for you. May I?" he asked, begging for permission to touch me.

I nodded desperately. "Please."

His hands were back on my skin, exploring with no barriers. The delicious friction of his rough calluses made me shiver. His fingers grazed the underside of my breast.

I yanked his mouth back to mine, ravenous, our fangs grazing. He palmed my breast, squeezing gently. I groaned into his mouth.

"You have no idea how much I've wanted this," he murmured.

"I think I have some sort of idea."

I grasped his waistband and pulled him with me, stepping toward the daybed. Sensing my intentions, he followed willingly, grabbing the back of my head with one hand while he lowered me onto the soft cushion, settling on top of me.

His mouth never left mine, his lips stroking, his tongue setting me aflame.

His hips settled between my spread thighs, our clothing doing little to disguise the hardness of his cock as it pressed into me. I shifted my hips, grinding against him. We both groaned at the friction.

"How about now? Will you bite me again, Redd? I want your fangs inside me, I want all of you inside me," I begged, grinding myself against his cock again.

He sighed, pulling his mouth from mine and gliding his fangs to the crook of my neck. "I could never say no to you, my sweet vampire."

I tipped my chin back, giving him as much space as possible, excitement thrumming in my veins.

"But not here."

Before I could question what he meant, he pressed a

quick kiss to the column of my throat before he lifted himself off of me, his mouth traveling to my collarbone, my breast. He scraped his fangs against my nipple, making me jerk before soothing the sting with his tongue.

"Oh!" I exclaimed, my body shocked by the sensation.

He continued his ministrations, moving onto my other breast until I was writhing beneath him, clutching his shoulders and begging for more friction. My hips churned uselessly beneath me.

"Patience," he chided me, biting the underside of my breast hard enough to draw blood. He lapped up the drop of blood that welled from my skin. Pleasure hummed through me. *More.*

I tried to be patient, but my body was screaming for more.

He slowly eased down my torso, fangs grazing a path across my sensitive skin. My body was wound tight enough to snap, the tension a delicious agony.

When he reached my center, he grazed his fangs over my clothed pussy, eliciting a shiver from my spine and a whine from my throat.

He unlaced my trousers and eased them down my legs, leaving me only in my undergarments.

He settled between my thighs, a smug look on his face, like he intended to stay there forever.

My desire was soaked through the fabric of my undergarments, my pussy throbbing. I was certain he could hear my pulse thudding beneath my delicate skin.

His breath fanned over my heated flesh, and I tensed in anticipation.

He inhaled, licking his fangs, staring at the fabric still covering me.

His hand slid up my thigh, slowly. His fingers paused when they reached the crease of my thigh, and I groaned in frustration. I was about to grab his hand myself when he suddenly gripped my upper thigh in a vice-like grip and sunk his fangs into my flesh, tearing into the pulsing vein running down my leg.

I screamed, a mixture of surprise and agonizing bliss, as my blood pumped into his mouth, and he swallowed me down. My spine bowed, my heels digging into the cushion to brace me against the onslaught of sensations.

He growled, deep and low in his throat, as he drank me in. Without removing his fangs from my thigh, he snarled and tore my undergarments from my body. The fabric chafed as it ripped away, a bite of pain that added to the mountain of sensations overwhelming me.

I was lost in the blissful torment of the moment, the smell of my own blood filling the air, mixing with his mint and sandalwood scent in a mind-numbingly perfect combination.

After countless moments, he yanked his fangs from my flesh, licked the wound clean, and shifted to my core without giving me a chance to breathe.

I squealed as his tongue stroked over my flesh, devouring me with no restraint. My back arched and I grasped tight handfuls of his hair, tugging at the roots. He growled deep in his throat.

"Yes. Yes. Holy fuck, yes," I panted. He held my hips down when I squirmed beneath him, keeping me still.

CHAPTER 39

Redd

Fiella was overwhelming my senses, the taste of her in my mouth, the smell of her perfuming the air, her sweet, sexy sounds filling my ears.

Her blood was swirling through me, filling me, intoxicating me, and I had to resist the urge to take even more. I flicked my tongue over her clit, relishing in her reaction as she twitched beneath me.

My cock was harder than it had ever been, throbbing in my trousers with a ferocity that was almost painful. Just the sight of her like this was almost enough to make me spend, and it took every ounce of self-control I had to keep myself contained.

I ravaged her with my mouth, paying attention to what made her body react the most, what made those delicious gasps and moans escape her lips.

I thrummed with primal satisfaction when her back bowed, and a choked scream scraped out of her throat. I held her down harder, unwilling to move from the paradise between her legs.

She pulled on my hair, feebly attempting to dislodge me.

"Give me one more, Fiella. You come so beautifully," I murmured against her soaked skin.

"Can't," She panted.

"I'm sure you can."

She pulled on my hair harder, wriggling away from me. "With you inside me. Please."

My eyes threatened to roll back in my head. With one last lingering kiss to her inner thigh, I reluctantly made my way back up her body.

Though her blood was swirling through my veins and lingering on my tongue, the urge to sink my fangs into her skin still tugged at me. I lingered at her neck, her pulse thumping wildly in her throat, her heart thundering. I dragged my lips over her throat as I settled over her body, and she tilted her head back in bliss.

"You're insatiable," Fiella laughed. "And still partially dressed, by the way. That's a problem."

I pressed a kiss to her collarbone as I pulled myself away from her. Her hands were quicker than mine, finding the buttons on my trousers and tugging them off.

"So bossy," I murmured.

"Shut up and kiss me," she retorted, feasting on my naked body with her eyes.

"Anything for you." I crawled back over top of her, relishing in the feel of her silky skin gliding against my own.

She looped her hand around the back of my neck and pulled my mouth down to hers as she wrapped her long legs around my hips. Her lips were hungry, insistent. She groaned at the taste of her own blood as my tongue slipped into her mouth, her grip on me tightening.

I slipped my hand under her ass, lining my cock up with her pussy. I thrust gently, once, twice, the underside of my cock rubbing against her dripping, hot flesh. She dug her heels into me, tilting her hips.

"Tease," she grumbled against my mouth.

"So impatient," I whispered, moving to kiss her jaw, her ear, her throat.

"I think we've both waited long enough."

"I couldn't agree more."

I pressed into her slowly, relishing in the feel of her scorching hot flesh, her body gripping mine. She dug her heels into me once again, writhing beneath me. We both groaned when my hips finally met hers, our bodies flush together.

I held my breath, fighting to keep control of my reactions. Her body was exquisite, made perfectly for mine.

"*Yesssss,*" she hissed through clenched teeth when I started moving.

I pumped into her slowly, savoring every inch of movement. I couldn't stop praises from falling from my lips. "You're perfect," I murmured as I picked up my pace, spurred on by her nails digging into my shoulders. "Absolutely perfect. The Gods couldn't have crafted a more lovely creature."

Somehow, Fiella's already flushed cheeks grew even darker. She let out a breathy chuckle.

I could tell by the tension in her jaw that she was clenching her teeth with a lot of force–her fangs looked elongated in the dim light. She was fighting her thirst.

A vision flashed through my mind of her teeth sinking into my flesh, of her sucking my blood into her mouth. An overwhelming wave of primal desire washed over me. I wanted my blood to be flowing through her veins as much as hers was flowing through mine.

I wanted us to be *one* in as many ways as possible.

"Fiella," I gritted out, fighting to keep my thoughts from swirling away into bliss as I pumped into her again and again. "I can tell that you're thirsty. Your fangs must be aching."

She shook her head, digging her nails into me even harder and swiping her tongue over her fangs. She winced at the action. "I'm fine."

"Fiella," I said again. I stopped moving, shifting my hand to grip her jaw. "You forget that I'm also a vampire. I know exactly how you're feeling right now. I've taken a lot of your blood, and you've tasted it on my lips. You can't suppress your instincts forever."

Her eyes dropped to my lips, and then to my throat, zeroing in on my pulsing jugular. She swallowed heavily. "But... it's not–"

I cut her off before she could continue. "We're way past that and you know it. Now I don't want anything about this moment to be tarnished by your thirst. I want you to feel as totally, completely, blissfully *good* as possible."

I released my grip on her jaw as I grasped her waist, flipping us over so she straddled me as I lay beneath her. I kept my cock buried deep inside her as I did so, unwilling to part for even a moment. The motion made her gasp, and her eyes closed for a moment before she forced them back open.

She looked conflicted, even as she leaned down closer

to me, drawn by urges out of her control. She set her hands on either side of my head. "Redd, I don't know, I–"

"Just bite me. I *want* you to."

Slowly, tentatively, she brushed her mouth against my throat. Her teeth grazing my skin made me shiver and my blood heated further, the desire nearly overwhelming me. I threaded my fingers into her hair, tugging her closer.

"Yes," I encouraged. "Just like that."

Her fangs cut through my skin like butter, the pain a short burst before the pleasure took over. My back bowed as my head tilted back, giving her unrestricted access to my vein.

She growled, the deep, animalistic rumble coming from the back of her throat. When my blood flooded her mouth, her restraint snapped.

She grasped my hair hard as she drank from me, yanking my head back even further. Her strength was impressive, but I could've dislodged her if I wanted to. I didn't.

I wouldn't dream of interrupting her. She was magnificent.

She became a predator, wild and unrestrained as she allowed her instincts to take over.

She ground her hips against me as she drank, writhing in an agonizingly perfect rhythm. I thought my heart would burst from the sheer pleasure of it all.

My balls ached fiercely, begging for release, but I held on for as long as I could.

I didn't want this to end a moment sooner than it needed to.

My vision blurred around the edges as she rode me into oblivion, my hips thrusting up to meet hers.

When she finally clenched around my cock, removing her fangs from my throat so she could throw her head back and let out a guttural cry, I couldn't hold back my release any longer.

Unending pleasure flooded me, waves and waves of bliss rendering me breathless. My heart thundered in my chest, so loud I could hardly hear anything else.

After the last waves of her orgasm passed through her shuddering body, Fiella sprawled on top of me, a boneless heap.

I ran my hand down her sweaty back, trying to calm my breathing as I came down from my high. I could smell my blood perfuming the air, the copper liquid still lingering on her lips.

My fingers slid over every knob of her spine, tracing her soft skin. She shivered when my hand glided over her nape.

"Holy fuck," I panted.

"I couldn't have said it better myself," she huffed back.

Fiella fell asleep quickly, her breathing evening out into a calm, soothing rhythm. I relished the peaceful, perfect moment, running my fingers through her snarled blue hair.

CHAPTER 40
Fiella

A light finger brushed delicately down my nose, over my lips, across my chin. I opened my eyes to see the setting sun gleaming through the windows. Hours had passed, but night had not yet fallen.

With a massive yawn, I rolled to face Redd. He was tracing his fingers over my face, looking content, if a bit tired.

"Good morning, sweets," he murmured.

I slapped his hand away with a laugh. "It's not morning, you idiot. Why did you let me fall asleep? The shop is still open!" I tried to sit up but realized that I was still as naked as the day I was born. I flushed.

He chuckled, pulling me back onto the daybed, tucking me sideways and curling his body around mine. I realized, disappointedly, that he was back in his clothes. Bummer.

"*One* of us really needed a nap. I made the rounds, making sure the doors were locked so we wouldn't get any surprise visitors."

"If you're talking about Sookie, the locked doors won't

keep her out," I mumbled sleepily, snuggling deeper into his embrace.

"I've been meaning to ask you about that. What's the story with the strange cats?" He tucked a strand of hair behind my ear, gently avoiding any tangles.

"I don't know, honestly. I don't ask any questions. It's more peaceful that way."

"Oh...kay. No questions about the potentially magical cats. That's fine with me."

I hummed in response, getting comfortable in his embrace.

Eventually, he broke the companionable silence. "Do we need to talk about this?"

I sighed, finally extracting myself from his arms. "Not now. Where the fuck are my clothes?"

He held my undergarments up, dangling them from his elegant fingers. "These? These are mine now." He tucked them into his pocket. "The rest of your things should be downstairs. Somewhere. You'll forgive me if I simply tossed them aside."

A flush crawled all the way up to my ears, my skin prickling with renewed desire.

"You sure did, didn't you. You beast."

"Beast?" he asked, brows raised.

He growled playfully, grabbing my waist and tossing me over his shoulder before eventually setting me on my feet.

"Okay, okay. Get yourself dressed and head home, we've still got a lot of work to do here," he declared while looking over his shoulder at the shop behind him.

I groaned. "Don't remind me."

~

It took some searching, but I eventually found all my clothes.

Redd and I lingered in the town square, appreciating the warming air and soaking up some of the dual suns' rays as we sat on a bench, shoulder to shoulder.

Critters scurried by without a care in the realms, the squirrels emerging from their burrows to enjoy the milder weather.

"So, we haven't really gotten the chance to talk much," Redd said, reaching over to tuck a strand of hair behind my ear. His fingers lingered, caressing the shell of my ear so gently it made me shiver. "I tried to see you as soon as I came back, but you weren't here. You know where I was, where did you run off to?"

I gasped, straightening with excitement. "Oh, gods! I can't believe I haven't told you yet! Kizzi and I traveled to figure out who sent those ghastly beetles after me."

His eyebrows rose. "Holy shit. And? Did you?" He hesitated for a minute, examining my face before smiling gently. "Of course you did, what am I even saying?"

I grinned at him. "I did. It wasn't your fault after all! I told you!"

"It wasn't, you're sure? How is that possible?" His eyes roamed over my face intently. "Tell me everything."

I was practically buzzing with anticipation. "I will, over a cider and a bowl of stew. It's a long story."

"Deal. Go home, change, do what you need to do, and meet me at Ginger's Pub in an hour." He stepped forward and planted a tender kiss on my forehead before stepping back again.

"Perfect, I'll see you there." I turned to depart, but his earlier words registered in my mind. "Don't think you're off the hook–I want to hear all about your spontaneous trip too."

He rolled his eyes playfully. "I'll be sure to tell you every boring detail, don't worry. I know how much you love a good story."

I smiled broadly, fangs flashing. "I would expect nothing less."

~

Today's cider flavor was strawberry basil. Not my *favorite*, but still incredibly delicious.

Redd didn't even hesitate when ordering himself his own cider–it seemed my superior preferences were rubbing off on him. As they should.

I absentmindedly pushed my salted rice around with my spoon as I explained my recent adventures. "It really went down as smoothly as I could have hoped. You know the other witches in town that Kizzi hangs around with?" I asked.

He nodded, swallowing a huge bite of buttery chicken. "Sure. I built a bookshelf for Ani's grimoires a few weeks ago. And I've helped a few of the others as well."

"Well, get this. Apparently, Kizzi has been working with the group of them, and they've been doing some investigating. Don't ask me for any details because the workings of the witchy mind are *way* too confusing for me to explain."

"Understandable. They're very smart ladies."

"Excuse you! I'm smart too, but I'll let that one slide. I know what you mean." I shot him a quick glare. "Like I was saying. They did a ritual on the beetles from my shop and traced the magical signature to another town!"

Redd looked impressed, his eyebrows quirking. "Wow, I didn't even know that was possible. Where did it come from?"

"Guess."

"Please don't make me," he deadpanned.

"Come on, guess!"

He stared at me blankly, taking a slow swallow of cider.

I snorted. "Fine, fine, you're no fun. It came from Willowvalley– that swampy, sludgy town that nobody goes to unless they must."

He set his goblet down with a thunk. "Huh. I don't know what I expected but it wasn't that."

"I know, right! What a stupid town."

"So, who was it?"

I groaned dramatically. "Well, remember how you thought this series of unfortunate events was somehow your fault?" I asked.

"Yes..."

"It turns out, it was actually my fault."

"Now how in the realms is it your fault? That makes no sense."

I braced myself to explain the repulsive creature that was Josten. I hated talking about that vile folk, but the story of his downfall was satisfying enough to make it worth it.

"So, there was this wizard that I used to know..." I

trailed off, unsure how to explain without sounding ridiculous.

"Wizard. Right."

"And he was behind all of it. *All* of it."

He nodded. "Sure. And why was some random wizard causing towns-wide destruction?"

I groaned. "He's my ex. We used to see each other, ages ago." I flapped my hand dismissively. "The details aren't important, but the root of it is, he was trying to get my attention with dark magic. But clearly, it spiraled out of control."

Redd had an incredulous expression on his face. "Holy shit. Seriously?"

I set my face in my hands. "I wish I was kidding. That jackass did all of this."

"And in Sunhaven? How did he cause those disasters too?"

"Well, you know how I told you I travel a lot to find trinkets to sell at my shop. I spent some time in Sunhaven during the early freeze season. He was trying to catch my attention there, too."

"That's... Wow. That's a lot."

"Exactly. So, at the end of the day, technically it is my fault. But if Josten wasn't such a raging idiot, none of it would have ever happened. So it's mainly his fault. He's in the Willowvalley dungeon, by the way."

Redd cracked his knuckles menacingly. "He better be..."

I snorted. "He is! The mayor said he'd be locked up for years. Decades, maybe. And the best part; his magic has been permanently stripped from him! He'll never cast a spell or perform a ritual ever again." I crossed my arms in smug satisfaction.

"I think he deserves a worse punishment, but I suppose that'll do."

"It'll do. Now let's hear about *your* trip."

We finished our meal together, exchanging stories and enjoying each other's company. I hadn't realized how much I missed him until he was back, and the hole he left was filled again.

On my way home, I dropped a letter into a mailbox and tried to suppress the strange surge of guilt that washed over me.

CHAPTER 41
Fiella

The next few days passed quickly, Redd's presence making the long hours feel shorter.

After a long day of assembling shelves, painting, cleaning up dust, and finding small tasks to keep ourselves busy, I found myself standing in front of Redd's cottage. I had walked over here with him under the guise of being curious about where he was staying, but really, I was just unwilling to part from him any sooner than I had to.

I was pretty sure that he felt the same way.

"By the way, I've been meaning to tell you. I'm thinking about planning some sort of grand re-opening for Fiella's Finds. It's common knowledge that things have been a nightmare in my neck of the woods, and I think folk will be too afraid to return until I scream in their faces that my shop is alive and well and I'm ready for customers!" I babbled.

"I think that's a great idea. We can pick up some pastries from the bakery in the morning, put a sign up, and make fliers to hand out in town," Redd answered. "But your customers will return anyway, Fiella. Folk love your shop and you know it."

I flushed, the flattery bringing warmth into my cheeks. "Yeah, well, it feels like the right thing to do. To embrace the situation and make an event out of it."

"It certainly couldn't hurt. I'll have some free time, if you need a helping hand."

I lingered for as long as I could, talking about anything and everything that was on my mind. Surprisingly, nothing about this situation felt awkward. If there was silence between us, it was peaceful. Comfortable. The two of us simply existing side by side.

But I couldn't quell the desire to get closer to him.

He looked incredible in the soft evening light, the dim glow of the moons and the stars glimmering off of his tanned skin and reflecting on his tousled hair. My fingers itched with the urge to tangle into that hair, to bury into the strands and hold on.

I ached for more, but he seemed content to just soak up the moment with me, his hands casually shoved into his pockets while mine practically vibrated with want.

Fine. If he won't make a move, then I will. I pressed up onto my toes, wrapped my arms around his neck, and pulled his lips down to mine. His reaction was instant. He grabbed my waist, yanking me even tighter to him, and kissed me back like he was drowning, and I was the air he needed to breathe.

His lips stroked against mine, his tongue smoothly entering my mouth to tease my tongue, my fangs. A shiver worked its way down my spine.

He seemed to absorb me into himself. I was melting and he was the only thing keeping me whole.

His hands tightened against my hips, his fingers flexing and digging into my flesh, almost hard enough to hurt, but not quite. I could feel his blood pounding in his veins, his heart thumping erratically, his skin growing flushed.

I wondered if he wanted to bite me as badly as I wanted to sink my fangs into him. I craved his blood with an intensity I couldn't wrap my mind around.

Gods, this man was an incredible kisser. I could kiss him for hours and never get tired of it.

I threaded my fingers into his hair, my nails scratching over his scalp. He groaned and his hands slid to my ass, grinding me into him.

I smiled against his mouth. That sound, gods that sound. I planned to coax it out of him over and over.

He lifted me and set me onto the edge of the dining table, stepping between my knees and closing the space between our hips. I could feel his arousal through the barriers of our clothes, his hard cock rubbing against me. Heat pooled in my core.

More.

His hands resumed their exploration of my body, touching, caressing, worshiping. One danced its way down over my thigh, to my knee, the other slipping to the nape of my neck to hold me in a possessive grip. In this moment, he had complete control over my body, and he knew it.

A whine escaped my throat when his teeth grazed my lip, the tiniest drop of blood welling up only to be stolen by the tip of his tongue. My muscles went lax, my body turning to liquid in his grip.

I leaned one of my hands onto the table to support myself and it landed on a pile of papers, immediately scattering the stack. The distraction was enough to momentarily clear my swirling thoughts.

"Oh shit, sorry," I broke the kiss and attempted to clean up the pile, the urge to organize briefly overtaking my thoughts. He'd never invite me back in if I trashed the place.

"Leave it," Redd mumbled, pulling me back. His mouth moved over my jaw, and he tilted my head, kissing my ear. Before my eyes could slide shut in bliss, I caught sight of the papers I had disrupted.

"Fiella, I couldn't care less about anything in the realm right now. All I can think about is you. Your mouth. Your skin. The way you smell. You consume me," Redd murmured into my ear. "Gods woman, you are *everything*."

I barely heard him, because my ears had started ringing.

I recognized that paper, that handwriting. Those letters. They were mine.

I fought to pull in air, my lungs refusing to cooperate.

Redd noticed my reaction and pulled back to examine my face.

"I didn't realize you were such a neat freak," he joked, until he realized the extent of the shock in my expression.

He picked up one of the letters. "Fiella, what's wrong? It's just paper. It's not breakable. We can sort everything into neat piles later if that would make you feel better."

I snatched the letter from his hand. I couldn't pull enough air into my lungs and all the blood had drained from my head. I was fighting the panic that threatened to overtake me. The room was starting to blur at the edges.

Impossible.

"Where did you get this?" I asked, slowly and deliberately.

"My mail? It was delivered. What do you mean, what's the problem?" he asked, bewildered.

I held the letter out of his grasp when he tried to reach for it again. "Where. Did. You. Get. This? Did you steal it? Is this some sort of sick joke?"

"No, I got it... I got it from the mailbox... Wait..." I could see the moment it clicked in his head, because his jaw dropped and all of the blood drained from his face, his skin turning a sickly pale color. "No fucking way."

"Where, Redd?" I asked, buzzing with a mix of emotions I couldn't decipher. Anger, betrayal, confusion, hope, something else that burned like acid.

He looked at me like I was a ghost.

"It's not possible."

"You're telling me!"

He stepped back from me like I had burned him. The space between us became a chasm, vast and uncrossable. I hastily hopped from the counter, straightening out my clothes and smoothing down my hair.

He began to pace back and forth, mumbling under his breath.

"It's *you*. It's been you. This whole gods damned time. Why didn't you say anything? What the fuck, Fiella!"

"Me?! What do you mean, me?! Why didn't *you* say anything?"

I didn't understand why *he* seemed shocked when *he* was the one who had been keeping this secret for weeks now! There was no way he didn't know. It was impossible.

He couldn't even seem to look me in the eye. I was sure

the guilt had to be eating him alive. To keep a secret so deep? So important? So all-encompassing? So life-changing? Diabolical.

On the other hand.... I hadn't managed to figure it out. The signs were all there, waiting to be recognized, but I had looked right past them. Maybe he had done the same.

I felt exposed. Vulnerable.

My thoughts were churning like the tides.

No wonder I found myself being pulled in two directions—the same enigmatic, alluring man was on both ends.

"Well, I don't know what in Hell's Realm we're supposed to do about this," I muttered awkwardly, hastily composing myself and pulling my cloak on. I ran my hands over my hair, trying to tuck the mussed strands back in place. I gave up after a few seconds and opted to pull my hood over my head instead.

There was nothing I could do to disguise the flush I was sure was staining my cheeks and the blood that I could feel pumping in my swollen lips. My body still thrummed with electricity, my skin begging to be touched. I pressed a hand over my mouth, and his eyes followed the motion.

He stood there frozen; a man wrecked.

What the fuck.

"Fiella, wait, let's just talk about this—"

I couldn't deal with this right now. I couldn't reconcile the idea of the penpal I had in my mind with the vampire standing in front of me.

I averted my gaze and slipped out of the door before Redd could say anything else, slamming it shut behind me and hauling ass away from the cottage.

The urge to flee was so strong I even forced myself to

run. Something close to panic was grabbing onto my chest. It wasn't a panic rooted in despair, more one grown from fear. From the unknown. From the potential for world-ending hurt this could cause me.

Kizzi's jaw was going to drop through the floor when I told her about *this* cauldron fire I'd gotten myself into.

CHAPTER 42
Redd

I stood in my kitchen, more confused than I had ever been in my life. Shock was making my brain slow, my thoughts sluggishly clicking into place.

I tried to calm my body's reaction, though blood still thundered in my veins and arousal still heated me. I took deep breaths, my teeth gritted.

Fiella. My penpal. Fiella *was* my penpal.

They were one in the same.

I struggled to reconcile the two folk into one in my mind, but the longer I sat in contemplation, the more the shock bled away and the joy crept in. All-encompassing and overwhelming.

I threw the door open, hoping to catch Fiella lingering, but all I could see was our footprints in the dirt—two sets leading toward the cottage, and one leading away, the steps further apart than before. Her intoxicating scent of warmth and berries lingered in the air. Strangely, her scent wasn't drifting towards town like I had expected but was instead crawling deeper into the woods.

I thought about going back inside and closing the door, giving Fiella a chance to sort her thoughts out on her own, but I threw that idea aside as soon as it formed.

This was *my* woman. Fiella was *mine*. And if she didn't see that yet, I would just have to find a way to convince her. To remind her. To *show* her.

I looked around suspiciously. I could hear the chattering of critters all around. I wasn't sure if any larger predators lurked in the darkness, but I wasn't willing to risk it. Fiella was too precious to me. Even though she could defend herself just fine, I couldn't suppress the urge to protect her. To seize her. To keep her to myself.

I took off, following the faint trail she had left, letting my nose and my instincts guide me.

I was a predator, and she was my prey.

I was going to catch my sweet vampire and make her mine.

Adrenaline flooded my body, tightening my muscles and focusing my senses until all I could smell, taste, and hear was Fiella. I was a beast on the hunt.

I caught a glimpse of her cloak fluttering around a tree trunk.

I picked up speed, zeroing in on my target. Leaves crushed under my feet and stray branches grabbed at me, but I paid them no mind. As I closed in on Fiella, I could hear her heart wildly thundering in her chest, her breaths sawing in and out of her mouth.

The urge to bite, to conquer, overwhelmed me. My fangs ached, saliva collecting in my mouth.

I grew closer, my legs pumping beneath me, the stray branches tearing at my clothes, at my arms.

She was almost within my reach now.

I called out to her when I was sure she could hear me over our footfalls. "Fiella, stop! If you keep running, I'll have to chase you. I can't help myself." The hunting instinct had its claws around my throat, the urge to capture undeniable.

She said nothing as she sprinted like her life depended on it, heading deeper and deeper into the woods. She somehow managed to pick up more speed as the seconds ticked by.

Her words eventually drifted back to me, carried on the wind as they escaped her mouth. "Catch me if you can."

I snarled, my fangs gnashing. *Mine.*

I could hear the distant sound of critters scurrying through the underbrush, desperate to escape our path of destruction as we tore deeper and deeper into the forest. My tunic grew damp from the dew on the leaves I tore past.

Though Fiella was fast, I was faster. I wanted it more—my urge to capture was stronger than her desire to escape. I closed in on her quickly.

My hand darted out, snatching the tail of her cloak, but she whipped it off before I could pull her back with it.

A dark, breathy laugh broke from her.

My little vampire was enjoying this. I smiled viciously. What an exquisite creature.

She darted around a tree and veered to the left, almost shaking me from her trail.

But not quite.

CHAPTER 43
Fiella

My heart was beating so fast I feared it might give out.

Adrenaline flooded my veins as I sprinted through the forest. Without my protective cloak, the tree branches tore at my skin, and I could smell my own blood perfuming the air.

I pushed my legs to go faster. Faster. Faster.

I resisted the urge to turn around, but I could feel Redd right behind me. He was impossibly fast. I could smell his sandalwood and mint scent drifting up to meet me.

I was being hunted.

I loved it.

Distantly, part of my mind screamed at me that I wanted to get away from Redd. That I was running from him for a reason. That I didn't want to be near him right now.

But the thrill of the chase ensnared me.

I ran harder.

I could sense Redd coming closer–could practically feel

his breath huffing against the back of my neck. I tried to feint left before darting to the right around an especially large tree trunk, but he anticipated the movement. He let out a feral growl of satisfaction as he closed in on me.

I screamed as Redd's arm snaked around my waist, snatching me off my feet before I could slip out of his grasp.

"*Fiella!*" he snarled in my ear as he hoisted me higher, pinning my arms to my sides as my feet dangled above the ground, kicking frantically. "Stop. Trying. To. Escape!"

I flailed uselessly. "Let me go!" I shouted.

"No. Not until you *talk* to me." He wrangled my body into submission, finally setting my feet back on the ground as he pressed my front into a tree trunk and pulled my arms behind my back. My cheek scuffed against the rough bark.

His breath heaved by my ear, his body pressing into mine.

I was trapped. Captured.

My heart was thumping wildly, my breaths sawing in and out of my throat. "I don't want to talk," I forced out through gritted teeth.

"Yes, you do. How do I know that? Because I know you, Fiella. I *know* you. Just like you know me."

I yanked on my arms, but his grip held, and he leaned more of his weight against me. My blood heated at his proximity, but my brain still held me back.

"No." I protested lamely.

"Yes. *Yes.* Just think about it. This isn't a betrayal. This isn't an act of deceit. This is *good*." He insisted.

I squeezed my eyes shut, my thoughts spiraling out of control. I had such a different relationship with Redd and my penpal. I struggled to reconcile the two.

"How didn't we know?" I demanded. "How didn't we figure it out?"

"I don't know," he sighed, leaning his forehead against my shoulder. "I didn't want to look too closely. I didn't want anything to change."

I groaned in dismay. "All this time, Redd. We were working side-by-side almost every day, barely tolerating each other."

"*I know*. I know."

"This whole time!"

"I know, Fiella!"

My anger boiled over, my frustration and confusion ripping through my control.

With as much speed and strength as I could muster, I whirled in his grasp, yanking my arms from his grip with a painful jerk of my shoulders. He didn't step back, and my hair snagged on the bark as he kept me caged against the tree.

"*Why won't you just let me go?*" I screamed, shoving against his chest.

He captured my hands, holding them against him with an iron grip. "*Because I fucking care about you, damn it*! I care about you *so* much. I can't stop thinking about you and it's driving me insane!" he roared, his face inches from mine. His eyes bored into me with enough heat to start a fire. "You are the *first* thing I think about when I wake up in the morning. You are the *last* thing I think about before I fall sleep. And it's *killing me*, not having you by my side every second of every day!"

Silence descended upon us—even the bugs chirping in

the night ceased their calls. The only sound was the thundering of our hearts, and the rasps of our breaths.

Minutes passed as we stared at each other. His grip on my wrists loosened.

Pieces clicked into place in my brain. The picture became clear.

"Say that again," I whispered.

"I care about you," He breathed. "I care about you, Fiella. I want you. I want to be with you. Gods, I just want to be *near* you. All the time. You have captured me—mind, body, and soul." He stayed where he was, caging me against the tree. My hands pressed harder into to his chest as we breathed in sync.

Slowly, the strange sense of guilt that had been clouding me began to drift away.

There was nothing to feel guilty about.

While I had been growing attached to my penpal, my friend, I had also been growing attached to Redd in the flesh. I craved his presence, I desired his company, I ached for his touch.

When I didn't say anything in response, Redd spoke again. "I know you care about me too."

"I do," I breathed, barely a whisper. Barely loud enough to be heard. He inhaled sharply, pressing ever so slightly closer to me.

"What was that? I couldn't hear you," he taunted.

I snorted. I spoke with more force this time. "I do. I care about you, too. More than I ever expected to. You've taken me by surprise."

His eyes crinkled at the corners. "See, it feels good to say it, doesn't it? It feels *right*."

I allowed his words to wash over me, the tension finally leaving my body. Desire took its place, thrumming through my veins. My heart quickened.

This vampire, this gorgeous, kind, helpful soul, could be *mine*. He wanted to be.

I slid my hands up his chest, over his shoulders, around to the back of his neck. He let me, his hands releasing my wrists and sliding around to my waist.

"Don't fight it. I know you're shocked right now. Hells, I'm shocked too. But this is *good*," he murmured.

I nodded. "It is," I said quietly. I pulled his head down to mine and pressed my lips to his. Hard. The lingering adrenaline of the chase reignited in my veins and heat pooled in my stomach.

His fingers dug into my waist, his grip tightening as he pulled me closer.

He deepened the kiss, his tongue sliding into my mouth in a caress that boiled my blood. I dug my fingers into his hair and relished his sharp intake of breath.

"Well," I murmured when I finally pulled away. His mouth traveled to my jaw before settling over my throat, his lips teasing my sensitive skin. "You caught me. What are you going to do with me now?"

He laughed wickedly against my skin. "I have a few ideas."

In a flash, he ducked, tearing my trousers from my legs with a harsh yank. I squealed in surprise. Before I could react further, he lifted me off my feet. I wrapped my legs around his waist on instinct. He kept my back shoved against the tree as he pressed his body into mine, erasing every inch between us.

"I hope there are no other folk around to hear," I gasped, winding my arms around his shoulders to help hold myself up.

"Let them listen. Let them hear you scream while I make you mine," he growled.

He dove back for my mouth in a frenzy, his fangs clashing against mine. He ground his clothed erection against my center, the heat radiating through the fabric. I moaned low in my throat.

"You know, that doesn't work so well with trousers on," I panted against his mouth.

I felt his smile against my mouth. "Patient as ever, I see."

He reached down with one hand to unbutton his trousers, only pulling them down far enough to free his cock.

Then he tore my undergarments from my body. I gasped in outrage. "Again? Seriously? You're going to need to buy me–"

"I'll buy you whatever you want, Fiella. I don't care about the gods' damned clothes." He brought his mouth back to mine as he lowered me onto his throbbing cock in one smooth motion.

He swallowed my sounds as I cried out, pleasure stabbing through me. He set a punishing rhythm, pounding into me as my back scraped against the rough bark of the tree. All I could do was hold on and take it, thoroughly enjoying every moment.

His hands held my hips with a strength that was sure to leave bruises, but I didn't mind in the slightest.

"You're mine. Say it," he gritted out.

I was too lost in bliss to speak, unable to form words.

"Fiella," he growled. He pulled out of me, and before I could protest, he set me on my feet and whirled me around. He pressed my front to the tree, pulled my arms behind my back, and entered me again in one sharp thrust. He resumed his agonizing rhythm, shoving me closer and closer towards a soul-rending orgasm.

He grasped both of my wrists in one hand, tugging just hard enough to arch my back. My shoulders stretched in protest. My breasts scraped against the tree bark, my tunic protecting me from any abrasions. The sensation only heightened my pleasure.

He pounded into me from behind. The sound of our skin meeting echoed throughout the forest.

"Mine," he insisted.

"Yours. I'm yours," I gasped.

"Good girl," he crooned, finally releasing my arms. I clutched the tree, holding myself steady against the onslaught of sensations Redd was wringing out of me. He reached around me, stroking my clit as his hips continued their delicious torment. I writhed, panting moans bursting out of me.

"Let me keep you," he groaned.

"Yes, please," I said, at his mercy. I would have agreed to anything he said at that moment.

His growl raised the hair on my arms, and I twisted my head to look at him over my shoulder, desperate to see his face. His expression was a mix of agony and bliss. Absolute torment.

"I can't hold on any longer, Fiella. You feel *incredible*. Come for me," he gritted out through clenched teeth.

His words were my undoing. I cried out as the orgasm

ripped through me, darkening my vision and turning my legs to liquid. Redd's grip was the only thing keeping me standing. I felt his hands tighten and his rhythm falter as he found his own oblivion, letting out a strangled groan that made me shiver.

When my vision finally cleared and I felt like I could stand on my own again, I pushed myself away from the tree.

His release dripped down my legs, onto the ground beneath me. I glanced at Redd, noticing that his eyes were on my legs as well. He swallowed harshly before tearing his gaze away and clearing his throat.

He tucked himself into his trousers, fastening the button before he spoke.

"I'm sorry about your clothes..." He mumbled.

I laughed, looking around helplessly at the dense forest surrounding us. "You should be! Now I've got to make it back to my cottage with my lady bits out on display! I don't even have my cloak."

Truly, the loss of clothes was worth it. We would probably pass my cloak on the journey back to town. I collected the tattered remains of my trousers and undergarments, clucking my tongue at the destruction. They would need to be repaired before they would stay on my body again.

The forest had come back to life, the critters resuming their chirping and the bugs restarting their chants. I shivered, the cool air chilling my sweat-streaked skin.

Somehow, Redd's cloak had remained fastened around his shoulders. He whipped it off and tucked it around me, scooping me up in his arms.

"Hey!" I protested weakly. "I can walk."

I didn't put up any real fight.

"I know you can," he laughed. He tucked me tight against his chest, one arm around my back while the other cradled my knees. "But I would like to carry you. I know how much you hate running, after all."

I snorted at that, settling into his embrace as he carried me back to his cottage, where I remained for the night, curled into his arms.

Where I belonged.

CHAPTER 44
Fiella

I sat on an uncomfortable stool in Kizzi's shop, teacup in hand, subtly trying to roll the tension from my shoulders. My night in the woods had ravaged me entirely, leaving me wrecked and aching in the best way possible.

Apparently, my stiffness wasn't as hidden as I had believed it was.

"Okay, I've been patient enough," Kizzi declared, setting the bowl she had been mixing down with a *thunk*, and hastily wiping her hands off on a cloth. "Spill, bitch. What the fuck happened to you last night? You look like you battled a wild bear."

I touched my face self-consciously. I had tried to cover up the scratches on my skin but there was only so much I could do. My sprint through the woods had left many marks on me.

"Girl, you better sit down for this one. It's juicy," I laughed.

I proceeded to tell Kizzi what happened, in tasteful secrecy (I told her every single detail).

By the time I was finished, Kizzi was clutching the table like it was the only thing keeping her upright. She looked absolutely scandalized. "Holy gods, you vampires are absolute animals." Her cheeks had flushed a darker green than I had ever seen them.

I laughed. "It comes with the territory." I nudged her shoulder. "You should find yourself a vampire man. I highly recommend it."

She made a fake gagging sound. "No, I think I'll pass on that one! I prefer my blood inside my veins, thank you very much." She glanced at me sidelong. "No offense."

"You don't *have* to let them bite you. It's just *extremely* fun if you do." I smiled broadly, flashing my fangs.

She covered her ears dramatically. "Gah! Enough! I've heard enough! You know I'm squeamish about blood."

"Which makes no sense, since witches use blood in spells and rituals all the time, but whatever you say," I muttered.

"That's completely different. That's work. Business as usual. Not..." She shivered. "I don't want to talk about it anymore. Next topic, please."

I acquiesced. "Let's talk business, then. How have things been here?"

"Absolute shit, now that you mention it!" Kizzi said. "All the folk in town needed me for a few weeks there while the madness was happening, but now," she shrugged. "Shit."

"At least the tourist season is coming soon! Will you have your wits about you when the influx of customers comes knocking at your door, or will the town be full of rainbow-haired folk?"

She sighed. "Gods, I hope I'll have everything in order." She looked around the shop with trepidation. "We took care of that asshole Josten, and things seem to have settled down, but I can still sense the sprites lurking around. They haven't set me free quite yet."

"Well, if there is anything I can do to help, I certainly owe you one."

"Damn right you do. I'm not sure if there is anything to be done right now. It seems like we're at a stalemate."

"Well, you better let me know if anything else pops up. You know I've got your back and I'll be pissed if you don't let me help you."

She flapped her hand. "Oh, shush. I'll let you know, Fi."

"To the moons!"

"To the suns!"

CHAPTER 45
Fiella

The next few weeks flew by as the weather slowly warmed, the mild season finally taking over Moonvale.

I traveled to all the closest towns, using all the silvers I had left to restock my shop and buy whatever I could find that was worthy of being on my shelves. Redd came with me when he could, but he occasionally had to stay behind to complete more of Mayor Tommins' tasks.

He was quickly becoming my favorite folk. Warmth bloomed in my chest whenever I thought of him. His smiles that were so precious. His giving heart. His caring attitude. His willingness to help.

While Redd wasn't obligated to do anything, I sensed that he had grown fond of the townsfolk, and he actually *wanted* to help everyone. He was stopping to chat instead of keeping his head down like he had when he first arrived in Moonvale.

The thought brought a smile to my face, my fangs flashing. I couldn't help but feel joy that my handsome vampire seemed to be settling into the town beautifully. The grump that I had first met had revealed himself to be so much more than just a scowling face. While he was still gruff and kept his emotions guarded, he was smiling more and more often, opening himself up. Making connections. Laying down roots.

I tried not to get my hopes up too high, but for the first time in ages, I felt happy. Truly happy. In a way that lightened the weight in my bones and made my spirit soar. I was quicker to laugh these days than I was to lash out.

Of course, I still lashed out when it was necessary, but that would never change.

Redd and I sat side by side in my shop–I was arranging a small shelf of trinkets while he was working on some sort of wooden sculpture.

"So, when do you think you're leaving again? To go back to Sunhaven?" I asked Redd, bracing myself for the answer.

He glanced at me sidelong, his eyebrows raised. He set down the wood he had been working with and brushed his hands off on his trousers.

"Fiella, sweets, it would take an entire army to pull me away from you. I am never leaving your side. Ever again." His eyes bored into mine. "Nothing in this realm could keep me away from you."

The words made butterflies take off in my stomach.

"Come on now," I shoved at him to try to make light of the situation. "You don't have to make any promises you can't keep. I'm a big girl, I can take it."

He caught my hand and clutched it in both of his own, rubbing his thumbs along my knuckles.

"I wouldn't lie to you, Fiella. Especially not about this. You mean everything to me. More than I can describe. I want you in my life permanently." His eyes seared into mine, his words caressing my soul.

"Wow, you really know how to sweet talk a lady."

He chuckled but squeezed my hand. "Come on, Fiella."

More seriously, I added, "You know, I guess you can start calling me Fi. I think you've earned it by now."

His eyes widened slightly. "Oh, wow, okay. I didn't think I'd get to this moment. Let me try it out." He cleared his throat. "Fi, my sweet vampire, I love you. With the entirety of my being. I can hardly remember the man I was before I met you. You have ensnared me, changed me, and forever altered my soul. Would you do me the honor of being my mate? Because I am yours, truly, entirely, completely."

My heart was beating faster than a hummingbird's wings. Joy fizzled in my brain, popping like bubbles. I didn't expect *that*. I never thought I would have a mate. Someone who I would tie my life to. Someone who I would weave into my very being.

Mate bonds weren't always forged between romantic couples, but when they were, they were eternal. The bond could be woven by a powerful witch, which would form a tie between the two souls. Forever.

The thought brought nothing but happiness. No hesitation. No trepidation. No fear.

"My dear Redd, nothing would make me happier," I

answered solemnly. "Yes, a million times yes. I love you, with all that I am and all that I ever will be."

We moved at the same time, clutching each other and pressing our lips together. The kiss was filled with passion, longing, and endless amounts of love. I couldn't pull him close enough, I itched to get closer.

Redd broke the kiss to tuck my head under his chin, hugging me so tightly that I could scarcely breathe. My ear was pressed to his throat, and his racing heartbeat under his skin soothed me. Easing my worries, smoothing my jagged nerves.

After long minutes, I finally spoke. "How are we going to do this?" I asked.

"Well, I'd like to stay here. In Moonvale, preferably."

"Great choice."

"With you, ideally."

"Naturally."

"You and I. Living together. In the same cottage."

"Of course."

He pulled back to examine my face. "You're not even arguing a little bit. Who are you and what have you done with my Fiella?" he joked.

I rolled my eyes. "I'd love to live with you. In my cottage, of course. Nowhere else would be acceptable."

He cracked a smile. "There she is."

I smiled back, both of us beaming at each other. "Of course, you won't really be able to change anything. I've spent ages perfecting it. I suppose I could clear out one corner for you."

He pulled me back to him. "One corner is perfect. As

long as I get to spend every moment by your side." He cocked his head to the side. "You do need a bigger bed, though."

"Good thing I know someone who can build one for me," I joked.

He snorted. "Good thing."

CHAPTER 46

Redd

That afternoon, I went by Mayor Tommins office to inquire about staying in town permanently. I shouldn't have been surprised, but I found myself taken aback when Tommins was on board in an instant.

He even had ideas for a business venture I could start up.

"You know, that old storage building behind the diner has seen better days. I don't even remember what was stored in there– it has been ages since anyone has actively used it. It's probably become more of a home for critters," he said. "What do you think about fixing it up and opening a shop there? The gods know that we could use a stable woodworking business around here."

I choked. "Tha–" I cleared my throat. "That would be amazing, boss. Yes. I'm in." I reached into my pocket to pull out my pouch of silvers. "How much is the title?"

He stopped me with a hand on my shoulder. "We'll get the paperwork sorted out later. For now, I just want to thank you for everything you've done for this town. Everything you've done for me." He looked more serious than I had ever seen him. Somewhere during our time together, we had become something close to friends.

"Of course, Tommins. You gave me somewhere to go when I was lost. You gave me a purpose, something to keep my hands busy. I owe you one." I shook my head. "Actually, I owe you *way* more than one."

He pulled me into a quick hug, clutching the back of my neck and thumping my back. When he pulled back, he smiled at me. "Welcome to Moonvale permanently, Redd. We are so glad to have you."

I grinned back at him, fangs flashing. "The honor is all mine."

CHAPTER 47
Fiella

The next few weeks passed in a whirlwind.

Redd and I stood, hand in hand, surrounded by witches in the town square. They gathered around us in a circle, their hands upon us, chanting quietly.

Magic hummed in the air. My hair floated around me as though caught in a sea breeze. My skin prickled with awareness. The scent of spring and fire surrounded us.

The ritual would bind our souls together, forever joining us. Linking us. Making us one.

We would be tied irrevocably and completely. If one of us passed to the afterworld, the other would follow. We would never be apart. Together until the end and afterward.

Redd and I were standing facing each other, a small cauldron boiling between our feet. He held my hands in a gentle but firm grip, grounding me. I squeezed his fingers in reassurance. He squeezed mine back.

I stared into his eyes and could see his love shining back at me. He glowed with life like never before, his happiness showing in the flush of his skin. He fought to keep the smile off his face, ever the stoic, but I could see the muscles in his cheeks twitching.

This was it. Redd and I, forever. As one.

I felt a brush against my ankles and looked down to see Sookie and her orange friend. The two cats were purring, butting us with their heads.

The chunky orange cat had been following Redd around more and more lately. I sensed a friendship forming.

Redd halfheartedly pulled his foot away from the critter, but it followed him, and he gave in, allowing the cat to claim his ankle as its own. I smiled.

As the ritual came to a crescendo, the magic in the air thickened. My hands grew clammy, a sweat breaking out over my skin. Redd rubbed his thumbs over my knuckles, the gesture familiar and comforting.

That's when I felt it. His soul inching closer to mine. His soul was warmth, and safety, and security. Spring and the tides. The power of the forest. The reassuring squeeze of a friend. My soul reached for his–a magnet. Undeniable.

The two were meant to be together.

My eyes fell shut. His soul caressed mine and then latched on. I heard his sharp inhale of breath as much as I felt it from within.

His essence overwhelmed me. Encompassed me. Filled me entirely.

It wasn't that I felt incomplete before, or like my being was missing anything, but once Redd's soul united with mine, any emptiness inside me was filled. It felt good. It felt *right.*

I pulled my eyes open to find that Redd was already staring down at me. Our eyes bore into each other, communicating things our words would never be able to say. I could feel his intentions, almost as though they were my own. He was happy. Happy wasn't a vast enough word for it. He was fulfilled. Complete. Overjoyed.

We were one.

Around us, the witches stopped chanting, and the town broke into applause.

I heard my best friend cheering the loudest, her voice booming over the crowd, and my smile grew so wide I feared my face would crack in half. My heart wasn't built to contain this much joy.

All I could focus on was Redd. He leaned forward, capturing my lips in a ferocious kiss. The sensation was different than before, and entirely overwhelming.

When we finally broke apart, Redd resting his forehead against mine, I finally registered the cheering around us. Our friends and neighbors were hooting and hollering.

"I think this calls for a drink!" Ginger's voice rang out over the noise.

The cheers became louder, and the crowd headed towards Ginger's Pub.

Redd and I lingered, soaking up the moment.

"Hello, my beautiful mate," Redd said quietly, caressing my cheek.

The suns were shining within my chest, warming me from the inside out. "Hi, mate."

"I would like to throw you over my shoulder and lock you in the cottage for the next few days, but I suppose we better go celebrate with the others." He gazed at me longingly.

I gulped, suppressing the shiver that tried to travel down my spine. "Well, we could ditch them."

He growled. "Don't tempt me, Fiella."

I laughed. "Okay fine. One drink, and then we'll slip out the back door."

"Fine," he sighed. "You better drink fast." His eyes raked over me, from my hairline to my toes and back up again. He licked his fangs. He grabbed my ass, squeezing hard. I squealed.

"Can you two cut that out? We're in public! Gods, I think I'm scarred for life," Kizzi shouted, stepping forward with her hand over her eyes.

I pulled away from Redd reluctantly, taking his hand in mine. "Don't be a hater, Kiz. We just love each other."

"Well, love each other a little less. Ugh. It's gross." She lowered her hand from her eyes and looked at us both skeptically before diving forward, throwing an arm around my waist and then around Redd's. She squeezed us tight. I wrapped my arm around her shoulders. Redd patted her awkwardly on the head.

Her voice wavered as she spoke. "I'm just so happy for you guys. Fiella, you're my best friend, and my favorite person in the whole realm, and I'm so glad you found someone who understands you *almost* as well as I do." She sniffed, her head buried between Redd and me. "And you, Redd, I wasn't sure about you at first because you were kind of an asshole, but you've really grown on me. But I'll scoop your eyeballs out with a spoon if you ever hurt my best friend. And I mean that." She squeezed harder for a moment before releasing us. She stepped back and dragged the back of her hand across her eyes, sniffing hard before composing herself. "Now let's go. Everyone's waiting for you."

My eyes welled with tears and my throat constricted. Redd and I shared a look. "Alright, let's go," he declared.

Before I could say anything in response to Kizzi, she whirled and sped toward the pub.

I had never seen the pub so packed. It seemed as though the entire town had shown up to celebrate the occasion. Folk were filling every table, every barstool, and had even overflowed onto the street. Everyone mingled, holding goblets and laughing.

Redd and I were intercepted every few steps with hugs, congratulations, and well wishes. So many smiling faces passed by that they began to blur together. Old Man Wilbur, Velline, Ani, Lunette, Tandor– *everyone* was here. My heart squeezed with a tender ache.

We eventually made it to the bar. Ginger sat down two of her largest goblets, full to the brim with cider.

"Bless you." I reached for the goblet gratefully. "I need this after all those conversations. I love this town, but I don't think I've ever hugged so many folk in one day!"

"Of course, honey." She patted my shoulder. "I made sure we had lavender blueberry for the occasion." She winked at me. "No other flavor would be acceptable today."

I had to swallow to keep my throat from tightening or my eyes from filling with tears. It was easy to forget that the people around me actually knew me and cared for me. The reminder was enough to catch me off guard.

Ginger nudged my shoulder. "You better not be getting soft on me." She smiled. "I just wanted my girl to have the perfect day." She grabbed Redd's shoulder too. "And her favorite guy too, of course."

He thanked her warmly.

After countless conversations, laughs, and smiles, the crowd began to thin.

A smooth voice filtered into my ears. A voice almost as familiar as my own, and one I hadn't heard in a long time.

"Fiella, my darling, you look beautiful!"

I turned to see my Ma standing in front of me. She looked exactly as she had the last time I saw her. Her silver-streaked golden hair was woven into an intricate braid, and her wrists jangled with a multitude of bracelets as she lifted her arms to wrap me in an embrace.

"Ma! What are you doing here?" My chin rested on her shoulder as she squeezed me tight. Her familiar strawberry smell made me smile. I caught sight of my father standing behind her. He was smiling broadly, his blunt human teeth gleaming. "And Pa! I didn't think you guys would come!" I had written them a few letters in the past weeks, informing them of the ceremony, but I hadn't heard back. I assumed they were traveling to the far reaches of the realm and hadn't received my messages.

I hugged my Pa next. "And miss our baby girl's mating ceremony? Never!" He ruffled my hair like he used to when I was a little.

I extracted myself from Pa's strong hug and pulled Redd forward. He smiled broadly. "Ma, Pa, this is Redd. My mate," I introduced him.

Redd stepped forward and took my Ma's hand, kissing

her knuckles fondly. She allowed the gesture and then pulled him into a hug. "Nice to meet you in person, Redd."

My Pa shook Redd's hand firmly, clasping his shoulder in a way that was surprisingly friendly.

"In person?" I looked between them confusedly. "What does that mean?"

"Your mate here has sent us a few letters." My Ma said, smiling at Redd. "He wanted to get to know us a bit, and to invite us to the ceremony. And the grand re-opening of your shop! Sorry we didn't respond to you, dear, we wanted it to be a surprise."

I looked at Redd with my jaw hanging. "You did?" My heart warmed at the thoughtful gesture. "You really think of everything, don't you."

"I had to introduce myself to the people who raised my sweet Fiella," he joked, tucking me into his side.

Another voice chimed in. "And we've been so excited to meet you, Fiella! We've heard *so* much about you!"

Redd released me and whirled around. "No way! Ma, you told me in your last letter that you couldn't make it with how busy the shop has become this season!"

"And miss my son's mating ceremony? Ha! We've been planning this with miss Fiella."

I smiled smugly. Redd wasn't the only one who could send secret letters. Redd's parents and brothers joined our circle, the family standing out with their suns-toasted complexions and dark, wavy hair.

"Woah, Redd, you didn't mention that she was taller than me!" Ollie exclaimed, sidling up next to me.

I scoffed and tilted my head down (more than was

necessary) to meet his eyes. "Are you intimidated, young vampire?"

He smiled good-naturedly. "Of course. You know Redd here had *lots* of nice things to say about you when he–" Redd cut him off by slipping an arm around his throat, pulling him into a headlock and rubbing his knuckles over the younger vampire's hair.

"Alright, alright, that's enough, bud. Don't go telling all my embarrassing secrets to my new mate after I've just locked her down." Redd said.

My parents and Redd's got along very well. Surprisingly so. We all lingered for what felt like hours, telling stories, getting to know each other, and just enjoying the company,

Redd couldn't keep his brothers' mouths shut for long, and my stomach ached from how hard I laughed at their stories. My favorite was about Redd trying to chase down their pet dog and ending up falling face-first into a pond.

After many, *many* more hugs and laughs, Redd and I extracted ourselves from the melee, sneaking back to my cottage hand-in-hand.

In the entryway, we ditched our cloaks and our boots. "So, mate," Redd said lowly. "We finally have some time to ourselves." He prowled towards me.

"It seems we do, mate." I backed away from him, a challenge.

He noticed my retreat and growled. As I turned to flee, he snatched me around the waist, throwing me over his shoulder. I squealed, kicking my feet and half-heartedly pounding on his back. "Let me down, you beast!" He swatted at my ass.

"Never." He slapped my ass again, harder this time. I

flinched, but heat spread throughout my stomach at the action. I stopped resisting, instead squirming against his hold.

He tossed me onto the bed on my back, immediately laying his body over mine.

"I'm building us that new bed tomorrow." He grumbled before pressing his lips to mine.

I wrapped my arms around his neck, arching into him. I mumbled against his mouth "We might as well wreck this one, then."

"You wicked, wicked creature. I like the way you think."

We didn't speak any more after that.

Epilogue

Later: Fiella

A book fell from the shelf on the far wall with a heavy *thunk*, startling me from my inventory notes. A small cloud of dust plumed in the air.

"Hey, knock it off, Pumpkin," I shouted. The mischievous orange cat had been coming around the shop a lot lately. I liked to think of him as Sookie's boyfriend, but I didn't dare say that out loud in her presence.

Sookie was a strong, independent lady cat who didn't need a man, and she made sure I remembered that.

As I glanced over my shoulder to glare at the trouble-making critter, I noticed that a piece of paper had fluttered to the floor and landed by my feet.

I smiled to myself. *Another letter from my mate.*

I snatched the paper off the rug and unfolded it, eagerly reading its contents before clutching it to my chest and letting out a deep, satisfied sigh. Redd sure had a way with words.

I gently tossed the letter onto the growing pile I kept in

a basket under my worktable. Redd and I had continued our handwritten correspondence, and every time I found one of his letters, my entire body flushed with warmth and my soul glowed with love. Nothing made me happier. Well... almost nothing. I supposed the letters could be topped by the vampire who wrote them.

I absentmindedly tucked my freshly colored blue hair behind my ear. I had grown fond of the color and had convinced Kizzi to brew me a bluebell tonic so I could keep the tint in my strands. This time, my nails had also turned blue, the color creeping up my fingertips. I wasn't upset about it.

Redd strolled in the door, two steaming mugs and a pastry pouch in hand. The scent of herbs and sugar filled the air, followed by mint and sandalwood.

"Oh, thank the gods," I called out, reaching toward the mug with both hands.

"Hello to you, too," he answered, holding the bounty out of my reach while he dropped a kiss onto my forehead. I tilted my head back, catching his lips in a quick kiss.

"I mean–hello, mate. I am thrilled to see you, as always. Thank you." I smiled.

"Much better," he teased. He finally placed the tea in my hands and the pouch of pastries on the counter.

Pumpkin rubbed against Redd's ankles, purring. Redd knelt down and scratched the cat's chin. He noticed the book on the floor, his letter on top of my pile. "That's a good boy, Pumpkin. Nicely done," he cooed.

"Meowwww!"

Redd straightened to his full height, brushing his knees off. "We've been working on that one for days now."

I rolled my eyes. "You trained the cat to deliver your letters for you? Unbelievable."

He grinned. "You're just mad that you didn't think of it first."

He wasn't wrong.

Laughing to myself, I turned back to my inventory notes. I had been working relentlessly, traveling to other towns to purchase knick knacks and getting everything in order for the Fiella's Finds grand re-opening. I needed it to be *perfect*. My parents had helped, as did Redd's family. We were splitting time between organizing my shop and refurbishing Redd's new warehouse.

The work never ended.

Though Redd and I both stayed busy, we always found time for each other.

I had been in desperate need of a boost when Redd appeared—he probably sensed my growing discomfort.

"So." Redd leaned against the work counter. "If I'm seeing this right, it looks like you're about done. Which means that you're ready for the shop re-opening tomorrow."

I sighed heavily. It felt as though there was still so much to do. My mental list was never ending. "Maybe."

"Relax. Breathe. You're ready. You can do this." He stepped behind me to massage the tension from my shoulders. "Now, eat your pastries and drink your tea. I'll help you finish up your inventory, and then let's get out of here."

I smiled. I would never grow tired of this. Of having my favorite person by my side. Forever.

"Deal."

My hands shook violently and a drop of sweat slid down my forehead as I stood at my counter in Fiella's Finds, preparing to officially open for the first time in months. There was an impressive crowd of folk gathering in the town square. I took slow, deep breaths.

Inhale, hold.

Exhale, hold.

I was nervous. Annoyingly, disgustingly nervous. I fought off the claws of panic as hard as I could, shoving them away with as much force as I could muster.

Redd sidled up next to me, gripping my hand and squeezing it tightly. "Breathe, Fi. You're ready. You know you're ready."

I exhaled harshly, clinging to his hand like a lifeline. "I am. I *am* ready. I don't know why I'm so scared. I've run this shop for years; this should be a breeze."

Redd nodded encouragingly. "You'll slip back into the rhythm. It will be as easy as breathing. I believe in you."

I squeezed his hand gratefully before letting go and stepping back. I fluffed my hair, straightened my overalls with a tug, and plastered what I hoped was a convincing smile onto my face. "Okay. Let's do this. You can let them in."

Redd smiled gently. "Yes, ma'am." He walked to the front door, turned the lock, and tossed it open wide. He held his arms out in a *come on in* gesture.

"Hey, move! Move! Me first!" I heard a voice shouting from a distance. My panicked smile morphed into a real one, my eyes pinching at the corners. Kizzi. My best friend was elbowing through the crowd, shoving past folk twice her size until she made it to the very front. She grinned at me as she strolled into Fiella's Finds, huffing and puffing. "Hey, Fi. Fancy seeing you here."

I laughed, rolling my eyes. "You didn't have to pummel my other customers, Kiz. There are plenty of trinkets to go around."

"I know, I know, but I wanted to be the first customer to shop in the new and improved Fiella's Finds. I deserve it, after all." She grabbed the first thing she could reach off the nearest shelf. It was a small, glossy black sphere on a wooden stand. She hardly glanced at it.

Kizzi strolled to the counter, bounty in hand, as other customers began to flood into the shop. *Oohs* and *aahs* could be heard from all around.

"I'll take this... thing, please. Whatever it is," Kizzi declared. She stuck her hand out, dropping two silver coins onto the countertop. I shoved them back at her immediately.

"I don't want your silvers! Just take it. Consider it my payment for your witchy services or consider it a thank you gift. I don't care. Just take it," I begged.

"Nope! You pay for your tonics; I pay for my trinkets. That's how it works. We support each other." She stepped back before I could reach out and shove the coins down the front of her smock.

"Fine," I grumbled, already making plans for how I would pay her back for all she had done for me. "You know I love you, right?"

"Of course!" she chirped before whirling around and slipping out the front door. "Moons!"

"Suns!" I shouted, though I wasn't sure she could hear me through the murmur of the crowd.

A line formed at the counter, folk excitedly purchasing their wares. A mild scuffle broke out in the sculpture section of the shop. A witch used her magic to pull the last wooden critter from a mothman's grasp. It landed delicately in her waiting hands. She chuckled, shrugging with false innocence. The mothman grumbled angrily but moved on, consoling himself with an ancient tome. A tall vampire with a broken fang watched the spectacle, his eyebrows raised and his jaw dropped in astonishment. *Redd's Pa.* I chuckled to myself.

It seemed that the folk of Moonvale had missed their trinkets.

Slowly but surely, the crowd worked its way through the shop, everyone finding a trinket that suited their fancy.

Redd's parents purchased a flowing tapestry that depicted a snowy landscape.

Velline found a painted stone bowl, so large she needed help to carry it back to Moonvale Medical.

Lunette bought a tall, gorgeous vase, enchanted to keep flowers alive for weeks instead of days.

My Ma found herself a small bracelet that was delicately hand-carved with swirls and sigils.

Pa grabbed a pair of teacups. They were made with steel instead of pottery so they would never break during travel.

Tandor purchased a collection of colorful, stained-glass tonic bottles.

Everyone purchased something. And everyone smiled as they left. My shelves were half empty by the time the last customer walked out the door.

All day, Redd stood in the corner, arms crossed over his chest, a slight smile lifting the corner of his mouth.

~

As evening fell, I sat at Ginger's pub with Kizzi and Redd, each of us with a cider in hand. Lavender blueberry, of course. My pouch of silvers sat heavily against my hip.

"Well, I'd say this day deserves a toast," Kizzi declared, lifting her goblet out in front of her. "To success, and happiness. And to my badass businesswoman best friend."

"I'll drink to that," Redd said warmly, clinking his goblet against Kizzi's. The two shared a smile before both taking a gulp.

I rolled my eyes, holding my own goblet out. "And to you two, because the gods know I wouldn't be here without you."

"Hells, I'll drink to that too!" Redd laughed. We all took another swallow.

"So," Kizzi mused. "How does it feel being mated? Think I'm cut out for the mate life?"

I laughed, glancing fondly at Redd before turning back to the witch. "It's better than I could possibly explain. Hells yeah, you're cut out for it. Everyone deserves to feel this happy. You just need to find someone who can handle you."

Kizzi scoffed in fake outrage. "Handle me? *Handle* me? Excuse you, Fi. That's rude."

I nudged her shoulder. "You know exactly what I meant. You need someone you won't squash like a bug."

"I suppose that is true..."

I was exhausted, and my cheeks ached from too many smiles, but my heart was fuller than it had ever been. I could feel the echoes of my mate's pride, his joy, his contentedness deep within my own chest. I glanced around at Ginger's Pub, at the familiar patrons, at the comforting atmosphere, at my two favorite people sitting next to me, and I finally felt whole. Completely, entirely whole.

All it took was a few anonymous letters and a mishap with thirst tonics.

Ani, the oldest witch in Moonvale, sat on a bench in the town square, shimmering magic swirling around her fingertips and coiling up her wrists. She had a hand-written sign clutched in her grasp and a self-satisfied smile on her face. Three cats sat perched beside her feet—one grey, one orange, and one striped. She leaned down and whispered to the critters, pausing to listen as they meowed back. She straightened, nodding.

Ani waited patiently, lingering on the bench until every folk was out of sight. When the coast was clear, she stood and approached the stone mailbox, humming a magical tune to herself as she did so.

Slowly, quietly, the magic in Moonvale was growing stronger.

THE END

Stay tuned for Kizzi's story next...

Acknowledgments

First, I want to say THANK YOU to YOU, reader. Thank you for taking a chance on a debut author and reading my book. It truly means the world to me. I've been telling myself for years, "I'm going to write a book someday..." and I finally did it. So thank you for picking it up.

HUGE shout out to my amazing cover artist, Žana Arnautović, for bringing my vision to life so beautifully. I hope my story does your art justice.

Mom- I couldn't have done this without you. You've supported me, cheered me on, and given me the tools and the courage to chase my dreams. Thank you.

Emily- You are my biggest inspiration, and I want to thank you for putting up with my endless questions and for encouraging me the entire way. Seeing you succeed has been incredibly motivational, thank you for lighting a fire under my feet.

To my friends and family, thank you for allowing me to become a homebody for the past few months in order to make this book happen, and for sticking by my side anyways. And to Laura, my own personal Kizzi. To the moons!

XOXO,
Hailey Blackwood

About the Author

Hailey Blackwood is a lover of all things fantasy- from cozy to dark and everywhere in between. She has always been an avid reader, but she is stepping into the author world with her debut novel, Love Letters and Thirst Tonics. When Hailey is not reading or writing, you will probably find her drinking tea (or wine) at home surrounded by her four cats and multitude of houseplants. She loves vampires, grumpy MMCs, and cozy fantasy worlds that you feel like you can step right into.

authorhaileyblackwood.com

instagram.com/authorhaileyblackwood
tiktok.com/@authorhaileyblackwood
amazon.com/author/haileyblackwood

www.ingramcontent.com/pod-product-compliance
Lightning Source LLC
Chambersburg PA
CBHW022103310726
48972CB00007B/1860